"What the hell are you doing here," Jordan Steele demanded, "taking another sabbatical from marriage?"

"Sabbatical?" Barrie's trembling hands clutched the doorknob behind her for support.

"Oh come now, Mrs. Wright," he scoffed. "We both know why you come to your little Oregon hideaway."

"I don't know what you're talking about! And it isn't Mrs. Wright, it's Barrie Coltrane. My...former husband and I...are divorced."

Jordan lifted a sardonic eyebrow. "Pardon me, but I do believe this is where I came in! Don't you think you should try to be a little more original this time around? Or have you forgotten I'm one to whom you've already told this little story?"

Dear Reader:

We've had thousands of wonderful surprises at SECOND CHANCE AT LOVE since we launched the line in June 1981.

We knew we were going to have to work hard to bring you the six best romances we could each month. We knew we were working with a talented, caring group of authors. But we *didn't* know we were going to receive such a warm and generous response from readers. So the thousands of wonderful surprises are in the form of letters from readers like you who've been kind with your praise, constructive and helpful with your suggestions. We read each letter...and take it seriously.

It's been a thrill to "meet" our readers, to discover that the people who read SECOND CHANCE AT LOVE novels and write to us about them are so remarkable. Our romances can only get better and better as we learn more and more about you, the reader, and what you like to read.

So, I hope you will continue to enjoy SECOND CHANCE AT LOVE and, if you haven't written to us before, please feel free to do so. If you have written, keep in touch.

With every good wish,

SECOND CHANCE AT LOVE Staff
The Berkley/Jove Publishing Group
200 Madison Avenue
New York, New York 10016

THE STEELE HEART
JOCELYN DAY

SECOND CHANCE AT LOVE
BOOK

THE STEELE HEART

Second Chance at Love books are published by
The Berkley/Jove Publishing Group
200 Madison Avenue, New York, NY 10016

THE STEELE HEART

chapter 1

BARRIE COLTRANE EASED her compact car into the narrow space between a big motor home and a pickup-camper rig parked at the cedar rail fence. The hot summer air smelled pleasantly of dust and pine and the smoky scent of a wood fire smoldering in the lakeside campground. The shrieks and squeals of children playing in the cold lake water drifted up from the shallow swimming area behind the store.

Barrie circled the length of the motor home, her steps momentarily arrested by the view of Mt. Hood looming in the distance. She supposed that someday she would become accustomed to the sight of the magnificent, snow-clad mountain, someday be able to look on the sight of the rocky crags and crevassed glaciers and majestic outline without a little catch in her breath. But not yet. It was too beautiful, always the same and yet ever changing. Fragile in the silvery light of dawn, massively handsome in blaze of midday, mystical at dusk. And often elusively reclusive behind a veil of haze or clouds. But today a mere wisp of cloud clung to the mountain's peak, an ethereal banner regally marking the lofty splendor of the highest peak in Oregon.

She walked behind the rail fence to the wooden steps of the small community's general store. She felt a quick lift of spirits when she saw that one of the two stained-glass pieces she had left on consignment in the store's cluttered gift and souvenir section had sold. The Mt. Hood scene,

of course. Maybe, just maybe, she would be able to make
a success of her stained-glass creations in spite of Killian's
disdainful dismissal of her work as a mere time-filling
hobby.

She picked up a yogurt and fresh tomatoes, frozen orange
juice and brown eggs, and carried them to the checkout
counter.

"Oh, there you are," Mrs. Peterson said gaily as she
punched a key to open the cash register drawer. "Your
mountain sold not over an hour ago. Two women from a
tour bus practically came to blows over which of them was
going to buy it." She handed over Barrie's portion of the
proceeds from the sale. "Will you have more pieces available soon?"

"The moving van with my sheets of stained glass and
worktable and other equipment is supposed to arrive some
time next week," Barrie explained. "I just happened to bring
these few small finished pieces with me in the car. But I'll
make up some more as soon as I can."

Mrs. Peterson rang up the grocery sale and deposited
Barrie's purchases in a paper bag. "Gorgeous day, isn't it?
Going to the open house this afternoon?"

Barrie rested the paper sack lightly on one hip. "What
open house is that?"

"It's that big new house on the far side of the lake from
you. The one with the peculiar-looking stuff on the roof and
all the windows." Mrs. Peterson rolled her eyes expres-
sively. "I wouldn't mind having what *that* place cost to
build. But I understand it's supposed to save money in the
long run. It's a solar house or whatever they're called."

"Yes, I thought it looked as if it had solar collector panels
on the roof," Barrie murmured. "Is the house for sale?"

"No, I don't think so." Mrs. Peterson, always busy,
industriously wiped the counter clean and straightened boxes
of chewing gum and candy. "It's just that everyone has been
so curious about the place. Maybe the owners decided they
might as well have an open house now so they won't be
bothered by snoopy visitors after they move in."

Barrie had been curious about the house too, intrigued
by the idea of a solar home in this area of the nation, noted

more for rain than sunshine. She had spent the last several days cleaning the old log cabin, and a break this afternoon would be pleasant. Instead of driving, she could hike around the end of the lake to see the house and get some exercise to work the kinks out of muscles sore from stooping and kneeling and stretching to scrub cupboards and corners.

Suddenly her attention was diverted by something more important. A gray-haired woman in a polyester pantsuit was carefully examining Barrie's stained-glass bluebird. Then the woman checked the hanging price tag and turned away, selecting an ashtray with a painted picture of the mountain instead. Barrie was disappointed but not really surprised. Because of the amount of handwork involved, plus the high cost of quality materials, the stained-glass piece was priced well above the cheaper souvenirs in the store.

"I might wander over that way sometime this afternoon, then," Barry said idly. And then again she might just stretch out in the sunshine beside the lake. She had better enjoy the luxury of these few days before the moving van arrived and she had to settle down to the serious business of trying to earn a living at what she knew was a shaky endeavor at best. To hear Killian talk, the idea of making a living with her stained-glass creations was pure folly, of course. Though probably no more of a folly than her plan to make the log cabin in Oregon her permanent home. The one time she had made the mistake of persuading Killian into vacationing in the cabin for a week, he had been annoyed with the cabin's lack of amenities, bored with the absence of social life, impressed by but quickly oblivious to the spectacular scenery, and restless because the entire week accomplished not one thing to further his political career. And how well any particular event or situation furthered his political career was the primary standard for judging its value for Killian, Barrie thought wryly. Except for Eleanor—

Quickly Barrie jerked her mind away from that line of thought. Whatever Killian did now, or had done in the past, no longer mattered. And if the truth were known, she thought with a peculiar pang, her past wasn't exactly lily-white either.

As if that vagrant thought had somehow affected the

present moment, she was suddenly aware of what Mrs. Peterson had just said. "Did you say the owner of the house is an architect?" she asked cautiously.

Mrs. Peterson nodded. "I hear he specializes in this solar type of house. Maybe he's on the right track. Lord knows we need to do something to keep our heating bills down, and sunshine is still free."

An architect. . . . Was it possible? Barrie struggled with a moment of pure panic. No, it was not possible. There must be dozens—hundreds—of architects in the state. The owner of the house across the lake couldn't be *him*. His home and offices had been down around Los Angeles, and she hadn't heard him express any particular interest in solar houses. Though not much of that incredible four days with Jordan Steele had been spent in conversation . . .

She shifted the grocery sack to her other hip and nervously rubbed a damp palm against her faded denim jeans. "Do you know his name?" she asked.

Mrs. Peterson shook her head. "Californian, I suppose." She said it with the grumpy disapproval of a former Californian who'd been an Oregonian for all of two years. "They're moving up here in droves, you know."

Barrie wasn't sure that was literally true, but the few people she had so far met here all seemed to have originated from somewhere other than Oregon. She suspected that some of Mrs. Peterson's disgruntlement came because many of the owners of the expensive new homes on the far side of the lake commuted to Portland jobs and didn't do a great deal of business in her store.

"Maybe I'll see you at the open house," Mrs. Peterson added. *"If* I can get Ralph to tend the store for a while."

Barrie swallowed nervously. "No, I don't think I'll be there after all. I—I have a lot of work to do."

Clutching her sack of groceries, Barrie turned and hurried to her car. She hadn't considered the possibility that Jordan Steele might be somewhere around the lake when she decided to come back here.

No, that wasn't true, she admitted a little wildly. She couldn't help but consider it, after what had happened here three years ago. But she had been so sure he wouldn't be here, *couldn't* be here. There was no reason for him to be here. He lived and worked in California, had merely been vacationing here in a cabin borrowed from a friend. And yet, even as she had assured herself back in Washington, D. C. that he couldn't possibly be here, some diabolically treacherous part of her mind and body had toyed with the tantalizing thought that he *could* show up at the lake again, vacationing at a more hospitable time of year.

No. It was preposterous, she decided firmly. She started the engine and shoved the gearshift into reverse, clashing gears in her nervousness. Actually, he hadn't really been vacationing here, she recalled. He wasn't happy with the architectural firm he was with and he had come up here to view the situation from a fresh perspective. Or something like that. He just hadn't talked that much about himself. And yet, for a brief period of time, she had thought she was in love with him. Maybe not so brief a time, she admitted reluctantly as the car bounced over the rutted road on this less populated side of the lake.

She parked the car at the rear of the cabin, unable to use the carport because of a sagging corner support post, another casualty of that unbelievable snowstorm three years ago. Darn! In her agitation she had forgotten to ask Mrs. Peterson if she knew of anyone locally to do some carpentry work. The sturdy log cabin was basically sound, but there were half a dozen minor repairs needed, and she had to have storage bins built for her sheets of stained glass.

She slid out of the car and went inside, opening and closing doors with more force than necessary, annoyed that she had let the mere mention of the word *architect* upset her. The owner of the house across the lake was no doubt a middle-aged Portland architect with a matronly wife and a flock of children to fill the big house.

Barrie decided to forego an afternoon of leisurely sun-bathing and threw herself into an orgy of window washing. Unfortunately, this activity gave her a rather frequent view of the comings and goings at the impressive house across the lake. Or perhaps that was exactly what her untrustworthy subconscious had in mind, she thought crossly as she gave up the effort to avoid looking directly at the house. She perched on the top of the stepladder and made a deliberately concentrated inspection of the angular, irregularly shaped structure. It was obviously not a typical suburban, rambling ranch-style home, but it had a classic elegance. It appeared to be built on several levels, and one section was almost completely glassed in. The exterior wood had a rich natural finish. Cedar or redwood, she guessed, though it was impossible to tell which from this distance. It also looked as if there was a skylight which just might be stained glass.

She tapped the spray can of window cleaner indecisively with her fingertips. She would like to see the house. This would probably be her only chance to see it, since she was hardly apt to travel in the same social circles as the owners of those expensive houses on the far side of the lake. And it would set her mind at ease if—no, *when,* she corrected firmly—*when* she found out the architect owner was not Jordan Steele.

She folded up the stepladder, nerves causing her to pinch her forefinger in the process, and went into the bedroom to change her clothes. She stood by the small closet sucking on the bruised finger and frowning slightly as she tried to decide what to wear, her slim body in strawberry pink panties and lacy bra a bit more voluptuous than her generally conservative clothing usually revealed. Shrugging, she yanked out a pair of designer jeans and a simple cotton gauze blouse with embroidered square neckline. She brushed her shoulder-length sable brown hair lightly and added a touch of glossy lipstick. Dampness had attacked the backing on the old dressing table mirror, and it gave back a distorted, wavy image that was not reassuring.

And why should she need reassurance, she reminded herself defiantly as she went out the back way. She was going to see the house, not to be looked at herself. She no longer need be so painfully aware of her image every time she encountered another human being. Or, to be more exact, she reminded herself grimly, how her appearance reflected on Killian's image.

The trail around the lake was popular with hikers from

the campground, and the dirt was powdery beneath Barrie's feet. She met several groups of hikers and exchanged friendly greetings. At the far end the path angled away from the water, circling behind a high, rocky outcropping that overlooked the deepest part of the lake. Here the trail led through a damp, shadowy glade where sunlight filtered among the entwined branches of douglas fir and cedar, and an impenetrable underbrush of vines and brambles created a living green tunnel along the trail. A narrow wooden footbridge arched over the creek supplying the lake. It would have been such fun to be a child here, she thought as she spied a spreading tree that practically demanded to be climbed.

On the far side of the lake, the trail ran only a few feet from the water's edge. Each lakeside residence was marked by a small boat dock, with a well-used path or elaborate steps running between house and dock. Except that the owner of the newly built house had not yet built either dock or trail, and Barrie found herself faced with the choice of using someone else's steps and awkwardly cutting through their yard or improvising her own trail to the new house. She chose the latter course and unhappily found herself floundering through thigh-high weeds and stickers, plus a shrub she fervently hoped was not poison oak. By the time she reached the driveway, her pants legs were covered with prickly weed seeds, her hair disheveled, her blouse snagged, and her arms scratched by blackberry vines.

Surveying the damage, she was tempted just to turn around and go home, but that certain stubborn side of her nature asserted itself. She picked out the weed seeds, ran her fingers through her hair to give it some semblance of order, and defiantly walked inside behind a casually well-dressed middle-aged couple who looked as if they could well afford half a dozen of the expensive homes on this side of the lake. Ignoring them, she now saw that the exterior of the house was definitely cedar. It still had a hint of fresh, woodsy scent.

Inside, Barrie forgot the other wandering sightseers in the pure delight of her own inspection of the house. The multilevel design was creative and there were several innovative features she did not fully understand, which evidently had to do with the solar energy aspect of the house, but there was no feeling of strangeness, of stepping into some impersonal futuristic world where beauty lost out to efficiency. The rooms were well proportioned and airy, with much open space and interestingly angled ceilings. Some of the walls were stark white, the perfect background for the artistically placed original oils in natural wood frames. Other walls, even part of one slanted ceiling, were a warm pine, and the stairway was lined with built-in wooden bookshelves. Windows revealed spectacular views of lake or mountain. Though the house was not yet furnished, one room had a telescope mounted for viewing the mountain.

Instead of a fireplace, the living room had a wide hearth on which stood an attractive cast-iron wood-burning stove with glass doors which would reveal flames flickering inside. Cozy and romantic as a fireplace might be, Barrie already knew it was also a terrible fuel waster and sent more heat up the chimney than into a room. The glass-fronted stove appeared to be an attractive alternative.

The glassed-in area along one side of the house, she now saw, was actually a greenhouse. It was built on a lower level but the glass roof extended above the dining area so that diners looked down on a lush enclosed garden of greenery. Upstairs she found that the skylight in the master bedroom was indeed a graceful abstract design of stained glass. The colored glass transformed the sunshine into rainbow jewels of light dancing on the walls. Outside was a small private deck from which her own rustic cabin was partially visible.

"Isn't this something?"

Barrie turned away from the deck's wooden railing and found the storekeeper, Mrs. Peterson, peering at her through the open door.

"I see you decided to come over and have a look after all," Mrs. Peterson observed. "Interesting to see how the other half lives once in a while, isn't it?"

"Yes, I suppose so," Barrie agreed lightly, wondering what Mrs. Peterson would think if she knew about the elegantly expensive home Barrie had left in Washington, D. C.

Back inside, a middle-aged man was explaining the workings of another skylight with louvers that opened and closed automatically by the heat of the sun. Barrie was relieved. He, evidently, was the architect-owner of the house. Just then one of the group asked that very question.

The man smiled. "No, I'm Hank Bevans, the builder. The owner—" The remainder of the answer was lost in the chatter of three children bounding noisily up the staircase.

Barrie's nerves, which had relaxed in her delight with the house, suddenly tensed into wiry knots again. The owner—what? An inexplicable sense of uneasiness dropped over her, palpable as a dark cloud, and suddenly she'd seen enough and wanted to start home. She edged toward the stairs with Mrs. Peterson following and chattering busily of remodeling plans for her living quarters behind the store.

Downstairs the curious crowd was thinning out. Barrie headed for the front entryway only to be stopped in her tracks by the sound of a male voice from the dining area. The voice was explaining the place of the greenhouse in the solar heating plan of the house.

"I still can't get it through my head just what the difference is between these passive and active solar systems I'm always hearing about," a woman's voice interrupted.

"Basically, though this is somewhat an oversimplification of course, a passive system is part of the inherent structural design and orientation of the house with its environment. Solar heat is caught and stored through the design of the house itself. The greenhouse is a passive system. An active system has various components or elements that operate more or less independently of the building. The solar collector panels on the roof are part of an active system. I feel the best designs incorporate both systems." The voice was modulated, patient but not condescending. "Some people find certain aspects of some solar designs less aesthetically pleasing than conventional housing, but I believe that our concept of what is beautiful may change as energy costs increase."

Barrie closed her eyes, swaying slightly. Even after three years, she instantly recognized the husky timbre of that voice, felt the shiver it sent up her spine. Slowly, she turned and looked in the direction from which the voice came.

The small group he had been addressing was moving toward the front door now. His back was to her, his broad shoulders and slim hips emphasized by plain dark slacks and white shirt. His brown hair, with just a hint of curl where it met his tanned neck, had glints of bronze.

"If we time it just right, maybe we'll get to meet the owner. I think that's him over there," Mrs. Peterson whispered. She paused, an odd expression on her face as she glanced at Barrie. "Or do you already know him?"

"Know him?" Barrie echoed faintly.

"You were looking at him as if you recognized him."

Yes, she knew him. She knew everything about him. She knew the feel of sinewy muscles in that powerful back naked under her caressing hands. She knew the sight and feel and scent of that lean, hard body from head to toe. She knew the warm curve of his body around her in the night and the laughter in his blue eyes when he looked down at her in the morning. She knew the intoxicating taste of his mouth and the way his kisses went from gently teasing caresses to deep thrusts of passion. She knew the throbbing hunger he aroused in her, and the powerful way he was capable of satisfying it...again...and again. The very memory sent a quiver through her, a remembrance that was half pain, half pleasure, leaving her knees weak and head strangely light.

And yet, paradoxically, she knew *nothing* about him. Nothing at all of the mundane, ordinary bits of information gathered over the time involved in the usual course of a relationship. Not where he was born or what his middle name was, whether he liked his steak well done or rare, how he felt about children or animals. And she didn't know how or why he was here...

She had to escape without meeting him face to face. She had to! He represented a four-day period in her life when logic, reality, the basic standards of her life, had been suspended. In their place was that erotic, sensual world in which only the two of them existed, a world imprisoned in a blinding snowstorm. She looked around, panicky. He was at the doorway now, shaking hands with people as they exited. If she had to touch his hand, look into his eyes—

"Are you all right?" Mrs. Peterson inquired. "You look a little flushed."

"I'm fine. Perhaps I got a little too warm hiking over here," Barrie improvised. She tried to calm her pulsing thoughts. Perhaps she was being foolish. Perhaps he wouldn't even remember her. Those four days had obviously been far less monumental in his life than in hers. But even if he didn't remember her, she couldn't face him. Maybe it would be even worse knowing those four days had meant so little to him that he *didn't* remember. She realized Mrs. Peterson was still waiting. "Oh, I just remembered. I wanted to—to see the kitchen again. You go on ahead."

Before Mrs. Peterson could insist on also seeing the kitchen again, Barrie turned and fled. The kitchen was empty of curious sightseers. Barrie paused, whirled indecisively, hardly seeing the gleaming metal of the built-in microwave oven or the warm wood cabinets. Surely there must be a back entrance. Yes. Through the utility room, a door that must lead to the garage.

She was yanking on the door, furiously refusing to believe it was locked, when a voice stopped her.

"I'm sorry, miss, but the garage is closed off. The contractor still has some equipment stored—" The friendly but authoritative voice stopped in mid-sentence as Barrie reluctantly turned to face him.

They stared at each other, the good-humored light in his blue eyes hardening to glacial ice with his instant recognition of her. There was not even a hint of uncertainty in his eyes. He knew exactly who she was.

"What the hell are you doing here?" he demanded.

"I came to see the house." Barrie lifted her head defiantly, her trembling hands clutching the doorknob behind her for support. "I didn't know you were the owner." Panic rising in her voice, she added accusingly, "I didn't know you were anywhere around here!"

"I see." He folded his arms against his chest and leaned

negligently against the gleaming white bulk of a washing machine. "Have you been here long?"

"Just a few days."

"Taking another sabbatical from marriage?" he inquired.

"Sabbatical?" Barrie repeated blankly.

"A time of rest. Leave of absence." His voice was maliciously pleasant. "A release from normal duties and responsibilities. A—"

"I know what the word means! I just don't see why you're applying it to me."

He was between her and the doorway to the kitchen, and she knew the casualness of his stance was deceptive. His gaze followed hers as she mentally measured the distance to escape. Deliberately he reached over and closed the door, imprisoning the two of them together in the compact room.

"Oh come now, Mrs. Wright," he scoffed. He smiled, a dazzling but humorless flash of white teeth against sun-darkened skin. "We both know why you came to your little Oregon hideaway."

"I don't know what you're talking about! And it isn't Mrs. Wright, it's Barrie Coltrane. My husband and I—my former husband and I—are divorced. I took back my maiden name."

He lifted a sardonic eyebrow. "Pardon me, but I do believe this is where I came in. Don't you think you should try to be a little more original this time around? Or have you forgotten I'm one to whom you've already told this little story?"

Barrie twisted the doorknob. Perhaps it was just stuck, not locked. He saw the surreptitious gesture and his chiseled mouth twisted into a faint smile. She gave up the effort. The door was locked. She took a step in his direction, trying to force a casual but firm air.

"If you'll excuse me—? I should be getting home."

He ignored her request, his eyes traveling over her as if he were critically inspecting some private bit of property for potential purchase. She felt her face color as the knowing gaze touched her breasts and waist and hips. She felt as exposed as if she stood naked before him. As she once had . . . though she hadn't felt exposed then . . .

"What happened to your arms?" he asked abruptly.

Barrie's precarious hold on self-control snapped. "I scratched them coming through your jungle of blackberry vines! Now if you'll just let me by—"

"Oh, but you were so anxious to go out the back way! Do let me help you." His voice oozed exaggerated politeness as he fished a key out of his pocket and reached around behind her to unlock the door. With conversational pleasantness, he added, "We locked the garage because the contractor still has some tools and equipment stored there."

Barrie barely heard him. Reaching for the door, his hand had accidentally, or deliberately, she hardly dared think which, brushed the rounded curve of her hip. Her flesh felt seared. She could feel the warmth of his body heat, smell the faint scent of his masculine aftershave lotion. She took a panicky step backward, flattening her back against the door.

"I can't open the door with you leaning against it," he said reasonably.

She glanced sideways over her shoulder. He was right. The door opened in. If she took so much as a step she would bump into the solid length of his body. A drop of nervous perspiration trickled between her breasts. There was a strange look in his blue eyes. Not the smoky blue warmth she remembered so well, but not glacial ice either. The moment was suspended in time, caught between the tick and tock of some cosmic clock.

"Jordan, I—"

Abruptly he stepped backward, opening a chasm of space between them, and the suspended eternity snapped. Awkwardly, Barrie stepped aside and he opened the door and she stepped into the garage, each of their movements elaborately orchestrated to avoid the slightest possibility of touching. In the dim light of the garage, Barrie saw a jumble of equipment, wheelbarrow, cement mixer, scraps of lumber, but the only thing that stood out clearly in her mind was the sleek yellow-and-black blaze of a snowmobile. She glanced at him, startled.

"Just in case," he said mockingly.

He opened the small side door of the garage and Barrie

fled without even an attempt at the polite convention of goodbyes. She was unmindful of the curious glances of a couple coming out the front way. She was on the paved road, walking at a furious pace, before she realized she had gone the wrong way and was now headed around the store end of the lake. Well, no matter. By now it was just as close to return home by that route as to turn around and go back. And she certainly did not want to pass by the house again and run the risk of encountering Jordan Steele once more.

Her mind was a seething cauldron of anger and hurt and humiliation as she tramped around the lake at breakneck speed. Sabbatical from marriage! Jordan obviously thought her brief but passionate relationship with him had been just some married woman's vacation fling.

But that wasn't fair! She had thought she was divorced when she met Jordan before; at least she was in the process of getting a divorce from Killian. She had filed for divorce... Well, at the time, she *thought* she had filed for divorce. Oh, it was all so complicated! Her mother had had no right to interfere. The anger Barrie had felt when she discovered what her mother had done suddenly stormed back, as violent as the original jolt of fury. But now, as then, the anger wilted into a sigh of regret. Under the circumstances, she probably would have dropped the divorce action anyway. Temporarily.

But she had written to Jordan, explaining everything, asking him to understand, and he hadn't even bothered to reply. She knew he had received the letter, because he had cashed the check she had enclosed. It had been a long time before she could bring herself to admit that what for her had been an experience that went beyond the physical had for him been merely an erotic interlude, interesting but unimportant. A titillating story with which to entertain his male friends, no doubt, every man's fantasy of being snowbound with someone else's oversexed wife. So how dare he act so self-righteous now, she wondered bitterly, her anger zeroing in on him again.

By the time she reached the store, she was hot, sweaty, and thirsty. Mrs. Peterson was already back at work. She cheerfully agreed when Barrie asked if she could buy a soft drink on credit since she hadn't any money with her.

"Well, what did you think of the solar house?" Mrs. Peterson asked conversationally as she busily refilled the cigarette display.

"I suppose it's all right. If you don't mind all that space to keep clean," Barrie said sourly. She was not about to rave over Jordan Steele's house.

"Did you meet Mr. Steele?"

"Briefly." Remembering Mrs. Peterson's earlier surprisingly perceptive comment about Barrie already knowing Jordan Steele, Barrie added, "He looks a little like someone I used to know."

"Did you meet his wife?"

"Wife?" The thud of Barrie's heart was so loud and erratic that she thought surely Mrs. Peterson must be aware of it. To hide her consternation she inspected the candy display with studied concentration. *Wife!* Until this very moment, the thought that Jordan might be married now had not even occurred to her. But how could it *not* occur to her, she wondered wildly. Jordan Steele was a handsome man, intelligent, charming . . . when he chose to be. And with a virile man's normal interest in women and sex. "Is he married?" she asked with carefully contrived casualness.

"Well, I don't know. I just supposed he was, with that big house and all. Looked like plenty of room for kids."

"No, I didn't meet a wife." And I couldn't care less whether or not one exists, Barrie added firmly to herself.

Barrie finished the soft drink and dropped the empty bottle into the wire basket by the counter. She intended to walk on home at a leisurely pace, but her feet seemed synchronized with the racing flight of her mind. Jordan Steele was *here,* acting as if he resented *her* being here, acting as if she had no right to be here. Treating her as if she were a—what? What exactly did he have in mind with his caustic "sabbatical from marriage" remark?

She was almost to the end of the campground before she realized she had again neglected to ask Mrs. Peterson about a local carpenter. She couldn't phone to ask because her telephone had not yet been installed. The old cabin had never had a telephone, so there were complications and delays because a trench had to be dug for the underground cable. She paused, thought about hiking back to the store, but decided against it. She was again hot, tired, and out of sorts. A swim was what she needed.

She went inside, stripped, and changed to a one-piece suit with a strategic wraparound design that emphasized the length of her slim legs. Quickly, almost running, she went down to the lake. She dove off a low rock and felt the initial icy shock as her body hit the water. She swam at the same furious pace as she had hiked, feeling a kind of frustrated anger that expressed itself in a need for release with violent physical action.

Finally she swam almost to the center of the lake in an efficient crawl stroke, then relaxed with a more leisurely backstroke on the return swim. She was an expert swimmer, the one physical activity at which she really excelled. Sports that involved balls or teams always seemed to take some sort of coordination or eye for distance that she did not possess. Killian had wanted her to learn golf so she could play with the wives of men he considered important, and she had doggedly tried to learn, but with little success. But swimming she loved.

Finally, as the sun sank and shadows lengthened across the water, she went inside. Her skin felt tingly as she dried off, and she realized she'd come very close to getting a burn from overexposure to the sun today. She fixed a fluffy omelet for supper and ate at the small dinette table by the window.

Across the lake, the new house was a blaze of lights. For the first time since coming to the cabin, she felt unaccountably lonely. Had she done the right thing, leaving behind everything familiar and coming out here to start a new life alone? She had no doubts about the rightness of the divorce, difficult as it had been for her to accept the end of what she had once considered a till-death-do-us-part commitment. The marriage had been over for months. No, it had been over far longer than that, she thought slowly. It was over when she and Killian had first separated three years ago, before she ever met Jordan Steele, and only circumstances had kept the false facade afloat.

But she could have settled for a less precarious existence than the one she had chosen by coming here. She could have lived with her mother, found some dull but secure office job, settled into a comfortable life surrounded by relatives and old friends in the quiet midwestern town where she was raised. And also enjoyed a certain amount of reflected importance as ex-wife of the district's congressman.

Instead, here she was in a rather run-down log cabin in Oregon, with no security except the six months' temporary alimony from Killian, and a determination to turn her artistic skill with stained glass into a worthwhile occupation. People were friendly enough, nodding or saying hello to her when they met in the store or post office, but she didn't really know anyone except Mrs. Peterson and a frisky chipmunk whose friendship she had cultivated with peanuts and sunflower seeds. *And* the neighbor across the lake with whom she had once had a brief but blazingly incandescent affair, she added as an unhappy afterthought.

Because that was all the relationship had ever amounted to, she reminded herself harshly. It wasn't some fateful, predestined meeting of two souls meant for each other as she had once dreamily and naively believed. It was just a wildly improbable four-day affair, strictly a product of circumstances. And sex. If they had met under different circumstances, they probably wouldn't have looked twice at each other.

No, that wasn't true, Barrie thought reluctantly, absentmindedly tapping the glass as her friendly chipmunk scurried along the window sill. She would have been sharply aware of Jordan Steele no matter what the circumstances of their meeting. There was his virile physical appeal, true. She couldn't discount that. But there was something beyond a raw sexual attraction...an authority, a competence, a strength to lean on, a feeling of dependable durability about him.

And just how did those noble characteristics correlate with the maliciously polite man she had encountered today, she asked herself wryly. The man who had never bothered to answer the letter in which she had poured out her heart.

She stood up abruptly and briskly carried her dishes to the sink. She was thinking too much. She had no doubt mentally enlarged Jordan Steele to some noble stature in order to relieve a subconscious guilt over the way she had tumbled into bed with him literally minutes after meeting him. No doubt the real Jordan Steele was the caustic man who had looked her over so brazenly today. With luck and a little determined effort, she could probably avoid seeing him for months on end even though they were across-the-lake neighbors.

She washed the dishes and rinsed out some underthings. The open house was evidently over now. The blaze of lights had dimmed to a muted glow from the lower-level windows. She switched on her black-and-white portable television, but the picture was fuzzy. Reception was poor in this area without a high outside antenna. She tried a paperback book, but it failed to hold her interest.

Finally, too restless to settle down, she slipped on a sweater and went outside. Typical of Oregon contrasts, the night was chilly in spite of the earlier heat of the day. Smoke from the campground drifted in a fragrant blue haze across the lake. There was the sound of laughter, a child's giggle, a man's hearty guffaw, that brought back Barrie's earlier feeling of loneliness.

She watched headlights bouncing along the rough road that bordered the campground. She expected them to turn in at the campground entrance, but they passed on by. That wasn't too unusual. Several times people had missed the campground entrance and come to Barrie's cabin at the end of the road before realizing their mistake.

This, however, was no pickup-camper, she realized as the car slid to a stop near her front door. It was a low-slung sports car, silvery in the glow from the living room lights she had left on. A man got out and strode purposefully toward the front steps.

Barrie felt a flicker of alarm. It couldn't be...

But it was. There was no mistaking that lean, formidable figure as he strode past the window, a scowl on his face.

Jordan Steele.

chapter 2

JORDAN'S DEMANDING KNOCK on the door could be heard clearly even from where Barrie stood in the dark shadows of the trees. Automatically she took a step forward, then checked herself. She was under no obligation to answer his knock, to submit herself to further humiliating taunts or questions.

She held herself rigid, almost without breathing, until his lean figure was momentarily silhouetted against the lighted window again. He slid into the low-slung car, and his annoyance was obvious in the way he revved the engine almost savagely. She let out her breath as the car backed in an arc around the front of the cabin.

A split second later Barrie realized she had miscalculated. She was going to be caught squarely in the glare of the headlights as he turned around! She dove for the shelter of a bush, but it was too late. The headlights trapped her in the incriminating position of a fleeing prowler. She felt utterly foolish, crouched there in the blinding glare of the headlights, her futile attempt to hide all too obvious. She shaded her eyes with one hand as she heard the car door open and close.

"Taking an evening stroll?" he asked dryly, a disembodied voice on the other side of the glare.

"Yes, as a matter of fact, that is exactly what I'm doing."

She squared her shoulders and moved out of the beam of the headlights, trying to ignore the embarrassment of the predicament in which he had trapped her. She *was* taking an evening stroll, or had been until he interrupted.

Finally he reached inside the car and switched off the headlights. "If you have a few minutes, I'd like to talk to you."

Barrie clutched the sweater uneasily around her slim figure. She shivered from something more than the cool night air. "I don't think we have anything to talk about."

"It's a business matter." His voice was flat and unemotional. "I was planning to write to you, but since you're here this will be more convenient."

"I see." She hesitated, uncertain. What possible business matter could they have to discuss? "I sent you a check to pay for the car rental and everything, but if it wasn't enough—"

"The check was quite sufficient." He sounded impatient, a little annoyed with her hesitation. "This is not a *personal* business matter," he added curtly. It was a deliberate emphasis that this visit signified no personal interest in her on his part.

"Oh. Well, won't you come inside then."

She led the way up the wooden steps and across the old-fashioned lean-to porch. Inside, she saw him take a quick, appraising glance around. She suddenly realized he had never been inside the cabin before. She wondered if he recognized it as a near replica of that other cabin they had shared for four days. His presence generated an electricity in the room that seemed to emphasize its shabbiness.

"It needs a few repairs," she said apologetically. "And some new furniture."

His aloof glance dismissed both the cabin and the modest furniture. The old blue sofa creaked slightly as he sat down on it. He had changed clothes and was now wearing a pair of faded blue Wranglers and a rust-colored velour pullover shirt. He looked ruggedly handsome, at ease and in control in spite of the awkward situation. A sharp contrast to the nervous tingles that made Barrie fuss around gathering up the book and newspapers she had been reading earlier. He started to unfold the paper he was carrying, then stopped. He took another, suddenly wary glance around.

"Are you here alone?"

"Yes, of course." Nervously she straightened the old lampshade that tended to droop on one side of the lamp. She would *have* to buy some new furniture. No, she wouldn't be needing it, she reminded herself. The living room was the only room large enough in the small cabin to use as a workroom.

Jordan's impersonal glance flicked back to her, his blue eyes meeting her brown eyes squarely for the first time since they had come inside. Something flickered behind that aloof blue gaze for a moment. A flash of remembrance that things had not always been so cool and formal between them? Then he briskly returned to unfolding the paper, and Barrie thought she must have imagined the brief flicker.

He spread the paper, a map, on the polished surface of the myrtlewood coffee table. The table was the one really nice piece of furniture in the room, a treasured reminder of a long-ago family trip to the southern Oregon coast.

He glanced up again, hand poised over the map, blue eyes completely impersonal. "I'm assuming you do own this property yourself?"

"Yes, I own the property," Barrie stated warily, somehow feeling she must be on guard. "It originally belonged to my father. He bought it with the intention of retiring here someday. I inherited it when he died. Though I really don't know what concern it is of yours," she added as a hostile afterthought, ignoring the fact that he had not asked for all that information. She did not interject the also irrelevant point that she had always doubted that her mother could ever be persuaded to leave family and friends in the Midwest for a permanent home in Oregon, and she suspected that her father had also come to that realization before his death. Knowing how much Barrie loved the cabin, he had left it to her rather than her mother, who would undoubtedly have disposed of it as quickly as possible.

"You don't need your husband's permission or agreement to sell the property, then?"

"I told you. We're divorced!"

"I was merely inquiring about the status of the *property*."

His faint smile, Barrie thought resentfully, came very close to being a sneer. A slow flush crept over her face, and she felt the humiliation of knowing she had again reacted as if she thought he had some personal interest in *her* status. An interest he was making a deliberate effort to emphasize did not exist.

"And just what is *your* interest in the property?" she challenged coolly. She straightened the persistently sagging lampshade again. She had the distinct feeling her hands would tremble if she did not keep them busy.

"I have a client, a Portland business executive, who is interested in building a home in this area. Your property would make an ideal site."

"You mean tear the cabin down?" Barrie whirled, her surprise overcome by indignation. "No! Whatever gave you the idea I was even interested in selling?"

"You rarely use the cabin," Jordan pointed out. "This is the first time you've been here in—" he hesitated almost imperceptibly "—in some three years."

"I have no intention of selling." She dropped to the edge of the blue overstuffed chair that did not quite match the blue of the sofa. "I plan to live here."

She caught the faint surprised lift of his eyebrows before his expression was totally under control again. It gave her a small, perverse surge of satisfaction that she could arouse *some* reaction in him.

"There must be many other suitable sites around the lake," she added.

"As a matter of fact, no. I've checked on everything on the other side of the lake. Most of the parcels are already built on, and the owners of those that are vacant aren't interested in selling. The campground takes up a good portion of this side of the lake, of course, and the land adjoining your property on one side is government owned." He eyed the map. "Actually, on this side of the lake, there's only your property plus the adjoining piece between you and the campground."

"Your friend owns that adjoining piece. Why don't you buy it?"

"I've already checked. He doesn't want to sell."

"I don't want to sell either," Barrie snapped. "I like my cabin, even if it isn't as . . . ostentatious as some of the places around the lake."

If he noticed the deliberate dig at him and his new home, he gave no indication of it. An uncalled for dig, she admitted guiltily. His home, elegant and beautifully functional, hardly deserved the derogatory term *ostentatious*. He smoothed the map.

"I thought you might be inclined to keep the cabin for—ah—personal reasons, so I brought along this map showing property locations and lines." When she made no move to do anything more than glance in the direction of the map from where she was sitting halfway across the room, he added, "If you would care to come over here where you could see the map—?"

Reluctantly she crossed the uncarpeted floor and leaned across the coffee table, hands carefully clutched behind her so there was no danger of touching him even by accident. Even no closer than this, she felt his nearness distracting and had to make a determined effort to concentrate on what he was saying. Out of the corner of her eye she noted that his strong left hand wore no wedding ring. She refused to let herself think that the small flutter that went through her was relief.

"This area here—" his forefinger outlined an irregular shape on the map, "—is your property. The cabin is about here." The forefinger stabbed a point near the edge of one property line. Barrie edged around the coffee table so that she wasn't looking at the map upside down, still keeping a careful space between them. "I've checked with the proper authorities, and it appears your property could be split into two parcels. So you could sell one at a very good price and still keep the cabin and a portion of the acreage for your own . . . purposes." He hesitated over the last word, as he had over *personal reasons*, and it came out with a mockingly insinuating inflection.

"My 'purpose' in keeping the cabin is because I love it and intend to live here," she reminded him sharply.

Jordan's slight smile was derisive, the faint lift of his

shoulders skeptical. "How you use the cabin is no concern of mine," he said smoothly. "I'm only concerned with acquiring a suitable property for my client. If you're open to an attractive offer—"

Barrie hesitated. The money from selling part of the property would certainly be useful. She could expand her limited supply of stained glass and make improvements on the cabin. The antiquated plumbing and electrical systems were both woefully inadequate. A little money in the bank would also give her a sense of financial security that she certainly lacked now. But what she liked about this side of the lake was the space and privacy, and she might need additional money later on even more than she did now.

"No, I don't think so," she said politely but firmly. "Thanks anyway, but I like the privacy of having a larger piece of land around the cabin."

"Yes, I'm sure privacy is extremely important to you."

The bitterness in his voice was so undisguised that Barrie was stunned. "Wh—what do you mean?" she faltered in bewilderment.

"Oh come on, Barrie." Jordan's chiseled mouth made a downward twist of disgust. "Don't be coy."

"I'm not being coy!" Barrie flared hotly. She jumped to her feet and faced him with dark eyes blazing at his veiled insinuations. "I just don't know what you're talking about. You seem to be implying that I keep the cabin as some sort of illicit hideaway for an occasional fling!"

"Don't you?" he challenged. He remained seated, unmoving except for the blue-steel eyes raking over her. "Isn't that what I was? A four-day fling to spice up your marriage, keep things from going stale? What is your arrangement with your husband—some sophisticated 'understanding' that you each do what you please while on separate vacations? Vacations that include not only a change of scenery but a change of bed partners as well? With some fairy tale about a divorce to soothe your innocent victim, of course."

"What I said about a divorce was true!" Barrie cried, brown eyes wide with shock at his ugly accusation. "And I wasn't here on a vacation—"

"No? That isn't the story I got from back east when I

called after you rushed out of here without even saying goodbye. According to the woman I talked to, you had returned from your 'vacation on the West Coast,' but you were 'out of town with Mr. Wright' at the moment. She said if I'd leave my number she'd ask you to return the call." His mimicking tone was devastating, then it hardened with scorn and disgust. "I told her just to skip it."

Who had he talked to, Barry wondered wildly. Her mother? Killian's sister or secretary? The part-time housekeeper? It had been such a confused time, days and nights running together in a blur of doctors and hospitals, the shocking revelation that the divorce was *not* in progress, the suffocating weight of guilt and responsibility. Yes, technically she had been "out of town" with Killian, because the hospital was outside Washington, and her absence at the time of the accident had eventually been passed off as a vacation. But it wasn't the way Jordan made it sound at all! She shook her head helplessly. "I wrote and explained everything."

"You call what you wrote me an *explanation?*" His voice dripped scorn and his clenched knuckles showed white against the gleaming table. "Perhaps your report to your husband of your little vacation adventure out here was more informative and exciting. What do you do—get together and compare notes on your conquests afterwards? I've heard about such cozy little arrangements, but they're just a bit too sophisticated for my taste."

Barrie had been preparing herself to explain it all again, searching for the right words to make him understand. But that final ugly accusation was too much. If the letter hadn't made him understand, surely nothing she could say now would.

Angrily she snatched up the map, haphazardly folded it into a crumpled rectangle, and thrust it at him. "Here! Take your map. I don't want to sell my cabin and I don't want to talk to you—about anything!" Desperately she fought to keep the tears that crowded her eyes from spilling down her cheeks. "Just go away!"

He made no move to take the map, just sat there looking at her with a strange expression on his face. She took a step forward to force the map on him, and in her blurry-eyed, chaotic state of mind her leg caught on the edge of the coffee table. She stumbled forward, tried to catch herself with an outflung arm, and plunged full length across both the sofa and Jordan.

She squeezed her eyes shut, trying to block out everything, as if by shutting it all out she could make nonexistent the terrible things he had just said and her clumsy fall and her tears and the agonizing memories and the unwanted thrill as she felt her breasts flattened awkwardly against his muscular thighs.

"Please, just—go away," she whispered, head turned away from his face. Her strength felt sapped, her muscles limp. The graceless fall seemed the last humiliation, more than she could bear. He had insulted her and she had responded by falling into his arms. She was aware of the inconsistency of her demand that he leave with her body still draped across his, and yet she hadn't the strength to extricate herself. The muscles of her neck seemed powerless to lift her head, and after a moment she felt the tentative touch of his hand softly smoothing the back of her hair. And deep inside she wondered despairingly if this wasn't exactly what that treacherous part of her subconscious wanted, if the fall was something less than a true accident.

After a moment he gently turned her over, shifting his weight so his arm cradled her shoulders. She had to open her eyes and look up at him. The changeable blue eyes were dark and brooding now. He caressed the wispy tendrils of curl at her hairline, seeming hardly to be aware of what he was doing.

"Why were you hiding from me tonight?" he asked.

"I wasn't hiding."

"Yes you were." The voice was soft but without a trace of doubt. "Why?" The wandering hand traced the curve of her jaw.

"I didn't feel like talking to anyone."

"To anyone? Or just me?"

"I—I don't know."

"You caught me by surprise at the house today." His voice sounded accusing but the fingers that smoothed her eyebrows were gentle. Her eyes drifted shut again, but without pain or humiliation this time. She gave herself up to the soothing, hypnotic touch of his hands, feeling as if she were floating defenseless on tranquil waters after a journey through perilous rapids. A forefinger outlined her mouth . . . exploring . . . remembering . . .

Something trembled within her, the tiny flicker of a flame she had thought long since dead. She was remembering too. . . . Remembering the solid curve of his ribcage and the reassuring thud of his heartbeat beneath the tentative exploration of her hand, remembering the rough, crinkly feel of hair on his powerful chest. . . . She twisted her finger around a curl of it hidden in the V neck of his pullover and felt the instantaneous quickening tempo of his heartbeat.

His hand slid lower, exploring her throat and then finding the curve of her breast in a caress that sent a sweet ache through her body. She had not put on a bra after the swim and she felt his sharp intake of breath as his hand closed around the softly yielding curve.

She opened her eyes and struggled to sit up, suddenly afraid. Of what? Him . . . herself . . . She brushed a stray strand of dark hair out of her eyes. "You couldn't have been any more surprised than I was," she said with a forced conversational brightness, incongruous with the intimacy of his hands still touching her. She struggled lightly again, but his arms were a velvet prison encircling and restraining her. She swallowed, feeling an almost uncontrollable desire to melt against him, to turn the clock back to the glorious, unrestrained passion of three years ago.

She gritted her teeth, dousing the hot flare of desire under a cold flood of reality. Sexual desire was deceptive, opening doors better left closed. "So, what are you doing here?" she added even more brightly.

"After you left, I waited around for a few days, until I got your check. And letter. When there didn't seem any point in waiting longer, I went back to California." His voice, though gruff, sounded a little less bitter and angry. "As you may remember, I wasn't happy with what I was doing there. I was working primarily with apartments and condominiums, and I was tired of just stacking people in higher and deeper, squeezing off a foot here, a foot there, to cut expenses for some developer. So I just junked it all and came up here and started my own firm, specializing in solar homes. For a while I thought maybe I'd made a mistake and I'd lose everything. Some people didn't believe solar homes *could* be successful here. But they are. And now everything seems to be working out fine."

"Evidently," Barrie murmured lightly, thinking of the new home and the expensive car parked outside. "I'm glad you're doing something you really want to do. That's very important."

She was still draped across his lap, her blouse twisted. There was a faraway look on his face that made her wonder if he was even aware he was still holding her. Then his hand slid down to the bare skin revealed by the twisted blouse and loose sweater, and she knew he was very much aware. She moved slightly and the grip tightened, not harshly, but with unmistakable reluctance to let her go. In the lamplight her skin had a pink-gold glow, product of a bit too much sunshine and a warmth that came from somewhere inside her in response to his touch. She waited, wondering.

The brooding look was still there in the small furrow between his eyes and the slight downturn of his mouth. "Are you really divorced this time?" he asked finally. "It's true?"

Barrie started to protest that it was true the other time too, but she was stopped by the complicated truth that, as it had turned out, it *hadn't been* true. In her mind she had three years ago bridged the painful gap between wife and ex-wife, or she could never have done what she did with Jordan. But the legal tie to Killian had remained unbroken.

"You really still don't believe that I am divorced?" she parried lightly.

"You must admit this all sounds like a rerun. And I'm not in the habit of getting involved with some other man's wife." His mouth tightened with a certain grim amusement. "At least not intentionally."

"Will you let me show you something?"

The slight scowl momentarily returned to his face, but then he shrugged and released her. She stood up and straightened her blouse, acutely aware of her breasts, naked under the gauzy material. It wasn't see-through material by any means, but neither was it totally concealing. And his touch had tautened the nipples to rigid, all too obvious peaks. Hastily she clutched the old sweater around her again and hurried into the bedroom.

She rummaged in the cardboard box of letters and papers until she found what she was looking for. She carried the sheets of crisp legal-size paper back to the living room and handed them to Jordan.

If she expected Jordan to exhibit some wildly joyous reaction, she was mistaken. He inspected the divorce papers carefully, not just glancing at them. He read every line, including the attached property-settlement agreement.

Barrie's nerves felt as if they were being tightened by invisible screws, stretched to the snapping point by his silent concentration. Why couldn't he just believe her? Why must she prove her status, like some errant child producing an excuse note from mother for teacher?

"Are you satisfied?" she snapped finally.

He set the papers on the myrtlewood coffee table beside the crumpled map. "You didn't get much in the divorce settlement," he observed. "What are your plans?"

"For several years I've been working with stained glass. Until now it has been more or less a hobby, but I'm hoping to turn it into a full-time occupation. I've done mostly small pieces designed to hang near a window where the light hits the glass. Mrs. Peterson has one of my bluebirds in her store. But I've also done a few windows and several entry-way panels." She paused and added tentatively, "I like your stained-glass skylight. I was a little surprised to see something that was added just for the beauty of it."

"Solar houses don't have to be ugly."

"I can see that now."

The conversation had suddenly become almost impersonal. Barrie gathered up the divorce papers, aware that in the quiet room their rattle revealed the nervous tremor of her hands.

"So I am divorced, you see," she said with a kind of forced bravado. "Quite free."

"No one is ever really free of the past." His voice and words sounded oddly somber, and Barrie glanced at him uneasily.

"No, I suppose not," she said finally.

"How do you propose handling your business?" he asked, abruptly changing the subject back to her work. "Place finished pieces in stores on consignment? Or do custom work on order?"

"If I'm going to make a living, I believe I'll have to do custom work on individual orders. But to get started I intend to make up some small pieces and leave them in gift shops or boutiques on consignment. I'm planning to go into Portland with some samples of my work as soon as the moving van arrives with my supplies and equipment, so I can make up a few pieces."

Jordan nodded. "That sounds like a good way to start." He stood up and reached for the map. He looked uncharacteristically indecisive, making no move toward the door.

"Thanks for the offer on my property," Barrie said awkwardly. "But I really do plan to live here and I don't want to sell."

He nodded again, absentmindedly. He walked to the door, paused with one hand on the knob. "When you're in Portland, why don't you give me a call at the office? I'm not living here at the lake yet. Perhaps we could get together for lunch."

Barrie's breath caught. "I—I'm not sure there's any point in that." Those were the words she said, but inside a different voice was trying to get out. *Tell me I'm wrong. Tell me there is some point in it. Tell me you want to see me again.*

He merely nodded slowly. "Perhaps you're right." There was no anger in his voice, only a kind of regretful heaviness.

And then he was gone. Barrie heard the car door slam, the engine start, the gravel crunch under the tires. She carried the divorce papers back to the cardboard box. She undressed and slipped into a short, pale lilac nightgown. Tears were not far away. She could feel them somewhere behind her eyes, poised like drops on the edge of a waterfall. She washed her face and briskly brushed her teeth, trying to dispel the cold, lonely feeling with her usual nighttime routine.

She felt vaguely let down, as if she had been holding her breath for an explosion and heard a pop instead. If he had stormed out when she had told him to go, she could now feel a certain righteous fury at his unfair accusations. She wouldn't be so painfully aware of the volatile chemistry that had always been there between them, a chemistry she knew he still felt too, however reluctantly. But now everything seemed so unresolved. He had indicated at least a small interest in seeing her again but had accepted without argument her halfhearted refusal.

She turned out the lights, but instead of slipping into bed she curled up in the blue chair by the window. Lights still shone in Jordan's house. As she watched, all but one went out. Only the light in the small but airy office, built on the same level as the greenhouse, remained.

Evidently he didn't feel sleepy either. What did Jordan Steele think about, alone at night, she wondered with a strange wistfulness. There was still so much she didn't know about him, and there was little chance that she would ever know any more than she did now. Did she even know herself?

How had she, Barrie Coltrane, an ordinary stars-in-her-eyes midwestern girl, with ordinary dreams of love and forever-and-ever marriage, turned into a twenty-seven-year-old divorcee who sat alone in an Oregon cabin on a moonless night, gazing across a lake at the window of a man who made her heart ache?

chapter 3

BARRIE WAS BORN and raised in the midwestern city that was the capital of her state. Her father was a high school football coach. Barrie suspected he was a little disappointed that he had no athletic son to follow in his footsteps, but he was always enthusiastic about Barrie's swimming ac complishments. Their home was only a block from the municipal pool, and Barrie practically lived there all summer, every summer.

When she was in junior high, her parents bought the Oregon cabin, and each summer the family spent several idyllic weeks boating, swimming, and fishing at the lake. At least for Barrie and her father the weeks were idyllic. Mrs. Coltrane was less enthralled by the cabin's rustic eccentricities.

After high school graduation, Barrie continued to live at home while attending business college. She got what everyone considered the glamour job of her class, working in the local office of the area's congressional representative.

Killian Wright was an aide to the congressman, running the home office and dashing around the state to represent him. The newspapers frequently used words like *brilliant* and *energetic* to describe Killian. They said he had "wit and flair and a political charisma of his own."

He had all that, of course, but Barrie fell in love with

him because he was fun and exciting, because he had an
offbeat sense of humor and interests that seemed breathlessly
wide-ranging. Also, as she unhappily realized much later,
all her friends were falling in love and getting married, and
it seemed the proper season of life for her to fall in love
too. She had a vague but pleasant image of life in a suburban
home with a couple of kids and dogs, family and old friends
comfortably nearby.

With the elder congressman's sudden massive heart attack, everything abruptly changed. Killian, already well
known in the state, ran in the primaries and easily won his
party's nomination. Two weeks before the big November
election, he and Barrie were wed in a big, splashy ceremony
given so much publicity by the local press that Barrie felt
almost overwhelmed.

Barrie's father was not totally enthusiastic about the
marriage, but he smilingly admitted he'd probably doubt
any man was good enough for his precious daughter. Mrs.
Coltrane had no such doubts. She and Killian got along
famously and she was ecstatic about the match. At the time,
Barrie did not attach any significance to Killian's choice of
date for the wedding other than to think privately that an
election campaign trip did not make for much of a honey-
moon. But later she was to look back with a much more
cynical eye and wonder if Killian hadn't timed the wedding
for its greatest political exploitation value.

In any case, he also won the November election easily,
and Barrie soon rather breathlessly found herself living in
Washington, D. C., as the wife of one of the country's most
promising freshmen representatives. Those first months for
Barrie were educational and terrifying, exhilarating and
nerve-racking and hectic. She felt so naive and unsophisticated, very much the "midwestern farm girl" even though
she had never in her life lived on a farm. Her smile and
friendliness and wholesome good looks didn't seem to count
for much in that sophisticated and cynical city.

Killian had an inborn sense of both political and social
survival, however, and under his strict tutelage Barrie shed
her farm girl image and began to earn a reputation as one

of Washington's brightest young hostesses. Together they were considered an up-and-coming couple.

Killian easily won reelection at the end of his first two-year term, but Barrie's disillusionment was already beginning. She was starting to find the social whirl shallow and meaningless, and she chafed under the restraint of considering every action, no matter how personal, for its effect on Killian's political career. His ability to laugh at himself had disappeared. Everything was deadly serious. The man she had fallen in love with had vanished behind a hard, polished gloss. She wanted a family but Killian said not yet, and she unhappily suspected any babies would have to be timed for the greatest political campaign value. She began to feel they hadn't a marriage so much as a political machine, and the machine's product was Killian, and it didn't matter if her values, her dreams, her basic individuality were mangled in the process. The death of her father was another numbing blow. She had never been able to talk to her mother the way she had to her father.

As a birthday gift, someone gave Barrie a precut stained glass kit for making a simple flower window hanging, and she found enormous pleasure in the small project. She quietly took an afternoon class in stained-glass technique and design and set up a workroom in the basement. This became her refuge, her private place where she could be herself, not constantly on stage representing Killian.

Killian ignored more than objected to her "little hobby," as he called it, so long as it didn't interfere with her real duties as wife and hostess. He disapproved when she had the temerity to replace a frosted window in the entryway with an unusual three-dimensional stained-glass scene. The window received many compliments, but Killian never priased her work or took it seriously. He also complained that she had changed too, from being vivacious and eager to stodgy and reclusive.

One thing Barrie never suspected Killian of, in spite of the disproportionate ratio of attractive, available women to men in the Washington area, was infidelity. They had a satisfactory if routine intimate life, and Killian was so wrapped up in his political ambitions that the idea he might risk the scandal of involvement with another woman never occurred to Barrie.

When she discovered he was involved with another woman, and had been for some time, her feelings were a confused jumble of pain and anger and bitterness and guilt. Pain at the betrayal. Anger at Killian over the blunt fact of the infidelity, anger at herself for being so naively blind. Bitterness because Killian obviously judged his personal actions on some cavalier standard far different from the rigid standards he set for her. Guilt because she felt she must have failed Killian or he wouldn't have turned to another woman.

Barrie packed a few things and went home to her mother to think things out. For the first few days she was confused and lost, but slowly she realized that beneath all her other feelings, under her dismal sense of failure as a woman and wife, was a growing feeling of relief. Whether she had married an illusion, or whether she or Killian—or both—had simply irrevocably changed, she could not say, but whatever they once had was gone. The fact of Killian's infidelity might have been the final breaking point, but the marriage had crumbled from within, weakened and cracked and broken in a myriad of ways long before Barrie knew about the other woman.

Barrie tried to explain some of this to her mother, but Mrs. Coltrane wouldn't or couldn't understand. She couldn't see beyond the fact that Barrie was throwing away a marriage to a man with such a brilliant future ahead of him. She wrung her hands and warned that Barrie would be alone and sorry later.

But Barrie knew the hollow loneliness that was *within* the marriage, and in spite of her mother's pleadings and warnings, she resolutely decided to file for divorce. She went to a man who had been family friend as well as family lawyer for years and started the legal proceedings. Afterward, Barrie decided to take refuge at the Oregon cabin for a few weeks until her mother accepted the situation. She tried to call Killian before she left, to tell him of her final decision, but he was out of town. Somehow she doubted that he would be devastated by getting the news directly from the lawyer.

Barrie flew to Portland and rented a car to drive to the cabin. An icy, sleeting rain was falling, and it turned to snow before she was out of the city. There were several inches of snow on the ground by the time she reached the cabin, near nightfall. She had never before been there in the winter, and in the falling snow the weathered old log cabin that she had always thought of as quaint looked tiny and dark and forlorn. Neither had she given any thought to the practical matters of light and heat. She found the electricity was shut off, and the heat supply consisted of a few chunks of damp wood for the fireplace. Already cold and weary, she realized she would have to drive back to the highway and locate a motel for the night.

Shivering, she returned to the car, and somehow, with the darkness and all-concealing layer of snow, she misjudged the driveway. The car slid into soft dirt and within moments the wheels were hopelessly buried. Then she had no choice but to stay the night.

The damp wood refused to burn and her supply of matches was soon used up. She ate a few bites of chili, unappetizingly cold, from a can she found in the kitchen. By flashlight, she located a few blankets and bundled up in them, indiscriminately cursing Killian, herself, the power company, the weather, and the rented car for putting her in this uncomfortable position.

She slept fitfully, fully dressed in an effort to keep warm, and woke every few minutes from the cold and the eerie sound of wind whipping around the cabin. With blankets still bundled around her, she finally stumbled shivering to a window and looked out on a world of ghostly, shadowed white. With a jolt of shock she suddenly realized her situation was not merely an inconvenience; it was critically dangerous. There was ice on the *inside* of the window panes, and her cold feet felt nerveless. Daylight was dark hours away. The snow was piling up with incredible speed, blowing into monster drifts and sifting through cracks around the window. Her fingers felt stiff and awkward. She had a sudden, terrifying vision of her body found frozen in the cabin days from now.

Panicky, she threw off the blankets, grabbed her purse, and stumbled on numbed feet to the door. On her way to the cabin, she had seen a dim light at a nearby cabin. Lights meant heat and safety, and she was beyond caring about the awkwardness of bursting in on strangers in the middle of the night.

She headed down the road . . . or at least what she thought was the road. In the windblown snow she quickly lost all sense of direction. A snow-laden bough snapped overhead, and a minor avalanche thundered down on her. In pure panic she realized her hasty decision to leave the protection of the cabin, however slight it was, had been disastrously wrong. She wandered helplessly through the drifting snow, falling, forcing herself to rise, feeling the cold creep through her body like a numbing drug.

When she finally came on a dark building, she thought it was her own cabin and tried to push the door open. It wouldn't give, and she pounded her gloved fists against it in a final burst of helpless frustration. Then she leaned weakly against the door, shivering uncontrollably, her mind as numb as her face and hands and feet, unable to think what to do next.

When the door opened, she tumbled stiffly inside, arms too weak even to shield her eyes against the blinding glare of a flashlight.

"What the hell . . ."

A male voice. A startled but strong, reassuring male voice. He shoved the door shut, then lifted and carried her into another room. She had a vague feeling of weightlessness in his arms, and then she was conscious of flickering fire-light . . . a voice talking to her as if she were a child . . . gentle, efficient hands tugging at her clothing. But still she was cold, so cold, and the shivering wouldn't stop. The dancing flames were no warmer than icy, faraway northern lights.

He helped her drink something hot to warm her from inside, and then there was another warmth encircling her . . . a secure, delicious heat that seeped through her naked skin with life-giving warmth. She snuggled into the comforting curve of warmth, too exhausted even to question its source. She slept with a dreamless sense of security she hadn't known in years, as if she had miraculously found some way to return to the warm security of the womb.

In the morning Barrie woke to find herself looking into the smoldering embers of an unfamiliar fireplace, and there was a male arm encircling her naked waist. And a distinctively male body curved spoon fashion around her body. She was, it appeared, snuggled into a sleeping bag with a strange man.

Strangely, after a moment of initial shock, Barrie felt no sense of alarm. Cautiously she twisted so she could look at him. He was still asleep, and she studied him openly. Thick brown hair, tousled with sleep. Tanned skin, strong mouth. It was all she could see of him in the intimacy of the sleeping bag, but she could feel that his body was lean and muscular. He moved in his sleep, throwing a possessive leg over her.

She lay perfectly still. Outside, the snow was still falling, and the silence, except for the small whisper of this unknown man's breath, was total. She felt no desire to move. She made no effort to analyze her strange reaction to the equally strange situation. She just lay there until suddenly she realized his eyes were open and he was studying her too.

"How are you this morning?"

"Fine . . . I think."

"I don't know much about hypothermia, but I think you were pretty close to it last night. I read that body heat is the best way to get a hypothermia victim warm."

"Thank you. I'm very . . . comfortable now." Their bodies were still intimately curved together.

"You stay in bed and keep warm. I'll get the fire built up and coffee started. The electricity is out." He started to slide out of the sleeping bag, then paused, his weight supported on one elbow. His tanned chest was only inches from her eyes. "By the way, I'm Jordan Steele."

"Barrie . . . Coltrane." She had decided to take back her maiden name, but this was the first time she had actually used it.

He had a magnificent male body, with long, sinewy muscles and lean hips. The line of tan ended at his waist and began again at his muscular thighs. He dressed with neither the undue haste of a man embarrassed by his body nor the elaborate slowness of an exhibitionist.

"Are you married?" Barrie asked.

He didn't seem to consider the question inappropriate or too personal. He turned to look at her as he tucked in his shirttail. "Not now." His blue eyes regarded her with open curiosity. "Are you?"

Barrie hesitated only momentarily. The legal divorce had only just begun, but in her heart the love was dead and the marriage over. "Not now," she echoed softly.

It was the beginning of four days that were a paradox for Barrie, an unreal, snowbound world of fantasy that was at the same time the most basic, natural thing she had ever known. There was no time for the usual courtesies or game-playing of a man and woman getting to know each other. They were trapped together in the cabin as the worst storm in twenty years battered the entire Northwest. The battery-operated radio issued a steady stream of reports of power outages and storm-related accidents and hardships and deaths. The city of Portland was at a near standstill, and the main east-west highway through the Columbia Gorge was blocked by snow. Here in the cabin they were no more than a mile from a store and highway, but they might as well have been on another planet. They were on their own, down to the basics of managing food and water and heat for survival.

The canned food supply was adequate. There was an overabundance of snow to melt into water. Heat was the crucial life-or-death problem. The supply of dry firewood was minimal, and Jordan rationed it out, carefully feeding in a dry stick at a time to keep the wet wood smoldering. But in the drafty old cabin the fireplace warmed only a semicircle in front of the rock hearth, and they ate and lived and slept within that small area of warmth. The basic effort for survival united them, and when the radio batteries failed on the second day, they were as alone as if they were the last two people on earth.

And the basic struggle for survival brought out other basic needs and instincts too. The first time they made love was perhaps only a raw physical need compounded of danger and the basic reaction of two healthy young bodies under constant intimate exposure to each other.

He came in soaking wet from trying to find firewood. She dried his wet, naked back. An exploding spark from the fireplace burned her neck, and she felt a strangely erotic tingle as his hands lifted her hair and sensitive fingertips applied salve. All day she was aware of a growing sexual tension between them, a humming electric undercurrent of male-female awareness.

There was no question about whether or not they would share the sleeping bag when darkness fell. It was the only way to keep warm. This time they both wore a light layer of clothing to bed, but when their bodies touched in the intimacy of the sleeping bag, it was as if the day had been one long prelude to love, a foreplay for the brief, fiery blaze of incandescent passion that engulfed them.

Barrie was stunned by the sharpness of the explosion within her body. It was as if before this moment that intimate part of her had been only half-awakened, half-alive. A flood-gate of repressed desire opened, a physical hunger she had never known before.

They made love again and Barrie didn't think it could possibly happen again, but it did. And this time there was the added sweetness of *time*, a leisurely climb through sensuous exploration to smoldering desire to blazing fulfillment. They slept with no barrier of clothing between them.

And somewhere in those four days, the sex became more than just a physical passion. It was a joining, a blending, a union into *one* that under normal circumstances might have taken weeks or months to accomplish. A oneness that some relationships never found . . . such as her own with Killian. But here it was all compressed into four days, just as their movements were compressed into that tiny semi-circle of warmth around the fireplace.

Barrie felt changed, metamorphosed from a dull, insensitive creature into a being of heightened awareness. Food had flavors she'd never noticed before, scents had a new sharpness . . . and sex, sex was an awakening to heights she'd never known existed. They explored and kissed and caressed each other with an unhurried sense that time would never end.

But, of course, it did . . .

Late on the fourth day, the storm broke and the sun glimmered weakly. By morning the sunshine was brilliant, and snow melted off the shingled roof in torrents of water. They could hear a snowplow working on the highway, but they knew it would not soon come to the cabin. The weight of the snow had collapsed part of the front porch, and Jordan set about trying to repair it. After lunch, Barrie reluctantly decided that she should hike to the store and telephone her mother, who was undoubtedly worried about her by now.

The snow was melting but the drifts were still treacherously deep. The going proved much more difficult than Barrie had anticipated. She was worn out by the time she floundered into the glassed-in phone booth outside the store. Phone lines were busy or down because of storm problems, and it took a while for the call to go through. When Barrie finally reached her mother, she was stunned to learn that Killian had been injured in a car accident and was in critical condition in a hospital just outside Washington. The doctors didn't know yet whether or not he'd live. Barrie *had* to come, Mrs. Coltrane said frantically. She sounded close to hysteria. Killian, when he was conscious, was asking for her.

Barrie felt a moment of frustrated anger. Always, *always* Killian was controlling her, forcing her in one way or another to do his will. Let his other women rush to his side! Then she was inundated with a flood of guilt and shame for thinking such a thing when he lay near death.

She told her mother she'd fly directly to Washington as soon as possible. Rapidly she reviewed her limited options. Hike back to the cabin to tell Jordan what had happened, hike out through the snow again, find someone to take her to the Portland airport.

No. She couldn't spare that much time. Killian's condition was too critical.

The noise of a big engine outside the phone booth interrupted her thoughts. A Greyhound bus was just pulling up to the store. The timing proved strangely fateful.

Rapidly she scribbled a note and left it with the storekeeper to give to Jordan. She told Jordan there was an emergency back east and she must leave immediately. She asked him to take care of returning the rented car for her and said she'd be in touch as soon as possible. She climbed aboard the bus only moments before the door hissed shut.

After a patched up cross-country flight, she arrived in Washington at dawn, haggard from lack of sleep. Mrs. Coltrane had not exaggerated the seriousness of Killian's condition. His sister, his only living close relative, was there. Mrs. Coltrane arrived a few hours after Barrie.

Mrs. Coltrane drew Barrie aside later that same day and gave her another jolt. She said she had been so certain Barrie was making a tragic mistake with the divorce and would regret her "hasty" decision, that she had persuaded the lawyer, as a personal friend, to delay starting the divorce proceedings. At this point there was no divorce, and Killian did not even know one was supposed to be under way. Mrs. Coltrane seemed to think the accident automatically canceled out whatever problems Barrie and Killian had had, and thus circumstances had proven her interfering action justified.

Barrie was dismayed and angry with her mother's interference, and the accident made no difference in the problems which had separated her from Killian. But the accident did change the situation drastically. She couldn't say anything to Killian in his present condition about a divorce, of course.

Barrie wrote Jordan a long letter, explaining everything, saying she would have to stay with Killian temporarily, and asking for his understanding. She gave him the telephone numbers at both the hospital and the house, and enclosed a check to take care of the car rental.

Jordan never called.

Barrie was too exhausted and worried about Killian to do more than think fleetingly of Jordan for the first few days, but by the time Killian's life was out of danger she had begun to worry about not hearing from Jordan. She checked both home and hospital. There had been numerous calls, but no Jordan Steele had left his name.

There was no place she could call him. She wrote again, sending the letter to General Delivery as before, but this one came back marked ADDRESSEE UNKNOWN. But she knew he had received the first letter because the check she sent him was processed through her bank account.

Barrie was stunned. She had fallen in love. Brief as their blazing relationship had been, she *loved* him. She had thought Jordan felt the same way.

But obviously he did not. How did he feel? What had he done with her letter? Tossed it in the wastebasket, appalled or amused that she thought four days in bed together really *meant* something? She felt humiliated and helpless and confused, as if the bottom had dropped out of everything. How could she have been so wrong about him? She had bared her innermost thoughts and emotions in those letters, and he hadn't even bothered to reply.

The only thing she could do was try to forget him. She no longer felt as she once had about Killian, but she did feel a strong sense of responsibility toward him. He faced a long, difficult recuperation.

Barrie had to respect the courage and determination with which Killian tackled his rehabilitation and grimly hung on to his position in the House. Doctors said he might never walk again, but he vowed he would, and in a few months he was out of the wheelchair and getting around on crutches. Barrie as resolutely tried to make a go of the marriage.

Killian's physical rehabilitation worked, but rehabilitation of the marriage did not. Barrie hung on for almost three years, partly out of that sense of responsibility, partly from sheer stubbornness, partly from the thought that Killian was trying to make the marriage work too.

She realized his effort was considerably less than total when she discovered he was again involved with another woman. And she was again shocked. Grimly she realized she would probably always be unsophisticated enough to be shocked by infidelity.

This time, however, Barrie did not rush off in hurt and confusion. She made careful plans. Killian again tried to persuade her to stay, but with cold clarity she realized he was more concerned about the possible effects of a divorce on his political situation than on the actual breakup of the marriage. When Barrie remained adamant, he did an abrupt about-face and said he would file for the divorce. Barrie did not question why. She simply assumed he saw some political advantage in handling the situation that way, and she didn't care. She just wanted out.

This time she methodically packed all her personal possessions, crated her stained-glass supplies and equipment, tied up the loose ends of her life in Washington, and planned for the future. She gave her mother no opportunity to interfere.

But Mrs. Coltrane's attitude seemed far different this time, and after a halting beginning, Barrie and her mother were able to talk as they never had before. Mrs. Coltrane said that at the time she had thought she was doing the right thing by interfering in the filing of the divorce, but she recognized now that her interference had only helped trap Barrie in three more years of unhappiness. She said the unhappiness showed in Barrie's face, and it hurt her to see it. She apologized profusely, begged Barrie to understand and forgive, and they wound up hugging and crying. She didn't want Barrie to move to Oregon, but she made no effort to stop her, saying she had interfered too much already and Barrie must live her own life.

Barrie was puzzled but relieved by her mother's change of heart and uncharacteristically effusive apologies. In spite of their new closeness, however, Barrie never told her mother about Jordan. She had never told anyone.

And that past relationship was a secret Jordan obviously preferred to keep far in the past.

Barrie stirred in the chair, her legs cramped and stiff from being too long in one position. She stood up and moved to the window. In the faint starlight, the mountain was a pale, luminescent shape, the lake a dark gulf of space. No lights shone from the house across the lake now, and the darkness seemed to emphasize the hollowness she felt inside. She thought she had gotten over Jordan Steele. What were four days out of a lifetime? But she knew now she wasn't over him. She had only buried her feelings deep in some hidden vault in her mind, and now the vault was open again, spilling out a tumultuous jumble of remembered passion...shared danger and laughter and warmth and intimacy...and the brutal rejection of silence.

The moving van arrived Monday morning, leaving a disarray of crates and bits of furniture and belongings. Her big worktable fit nicely under the window facing the lake, and she dug out her tools and enough stained glass to get started on some sample pieces to take into Portland. She decided initially to concentrate on simple Mt. Hood window hangings that could be priced relatively low.

When her thoughts strayed to Jordan, as they all too often did, she resolutely forced them away. Seeing him again had reawakened old feelings, but she had buried those feelings once and she must do it again.

By late afternoon, Barrie had discovered that working in the clear natural light of the cabin was far superior to the artificial light in the basement of the Washington house. Less satisfactory were her encounters with the cabin's inadequate and antiquated electrical system. She soon discovered that the small soldering iron she used in her work, if used when other electrical appliances were running, was just enough to blow a fuse.

Out of fuses and with back aching from bending over the worktable all day, she decided to hike to the store. This time she remembered to check the bulletin board and found the name and phone number of a man advertising carpentry work. She telephoned him, and he said he'd come around later in the week.

Inside the store, she bought fuses and was pleasantly surprised to find her stained-glass bluebird had been sold. She was even more surprised when Mrs. Peterson said Jordan Steele was the buyer.

Why had he done it?

She pondered the question off and on all week, reading

first one bit of significance into the action, and then another. One thing she knew: it was not simply a casual, spur-of-the-moment purchase. It was a deliberate action.

The carpenter came by on Thursday afternoon. He introduced himself as Mike Setlow. He was young, brawny, and outgoing. She liked him immediately in spite of his quick, cheerful conclusion that the cabin was a "carpenter's, plumber's, and electrician's collaboration on a nightmare." He was a college student, working for himself during the summer. Barrie pointed out repairs she wanted made and described the type of bins she needed for her sheets of stained glass and the lead came, the metal strips used to encircle each piece of cut glass and join it to the others in a design.

Mike hung around for quite a while, his interest in Barrie obviously more than a business matter. Finally he suggested they drive into town in his old pickup and have pizza together for dinner.

Barrie hesitated. He was so *young*.

Reading her mind, he said, "I'm twenty-four. Late starter at college. Which makes me—" he squinted speculatively at her "—all of a year or two younger than you."

"Three," Barrie corrected. "And I'm divorced."

"Lordy me," he said, rolling his eyes in grossly exaggerated shock. "A twenty-seven-year-old *divorcee*."

He was gently making fun of her, and Barrie had to laugh at herself too. He was not, after all, suggesting a lifetime commitment, just pizza. What did age matter?

Barrie enjoyed the pizza and Mike's light, cheerful banter. He was a pleasant antidote for the dispirited, lonely feelings she'd been fighting lately. He said he'd be back sometime the following week to start work on her storage bins and repairs.

Barrie worked steadily, straight through the weekend, taking extra pains to make each cut exact, each soldered joint smooth and even. The weather was gloriously perfect, and she relaxed with a swim each afternoon. Her telephone still had not been installed, though she saw a phone company truck at Jordan's house across the lake. Try as she might,

her will power was never quite strong enough to keep her
from glancing in that direction every now and then through-
out the day.

On Saturday evening there were lights on at his house.
On Sunday Jordan hacked a path from the house down to
the lake trail. Even at that distance, Barrie could tell it was
he. He wielded the flashing blade as if it were a weapon,
savagely slashing at the tangled brush and brambles. She
stayed inside, skipping her usual swim. He had made no
effort to see her, and she would not cavort around the water
as if she were trying to attract his attention.

By midweek, Barrie had half a dozen of the Mt. Hood
window hangings completed, plus a couple of flower designs. Armed with those, and several display folders with
photographs of other, more complicated pieces she had done
in the past, she felt ready to tackle Portland with her wares.

She was nervous as she headed toward Portland early
Wednesday morning. What if no one was interested? What
if she couldn't sell *anything?* What if—? A dozen dismal
possibilities presented themselves.

Her nervous fears proved unfounded. A few places
weren't interested in stained-glass work, and a couple of
others were already supplied with stained-glass pieces created by other local craftsmen. But others readily agreed to
take the single pieces she offered on consignment and were
interested in carrying more of her work. One store owner
said she would give Barrie's name to a client who was
planning a large opaque glass window for a bathroom remodeling project. Barrie's spirits soared when, right while
she was showing her last Mt. Hood window hanging, a
customer wanted to buy it. Her work could hardly have
found a better recommendation, and the store placed a definite order for half a dozen more pieces. It was by no means
a living yet, but it was a start.

She glanced at her watch as she returned to her car.
Quarter to one. She hadn't had lunch yet. If she hurried
home, she could get to work on the new order. But she
didn't feel like hurrying home. The day was glorious. Even
Mt. Hood was out from behind the haze or clouds that often
obscured it from Portland, and it rose above its surroundings

in majestic splendor. She felt exhilarated, like a gambler on a winning streak. She wanted to shout her good news and celebrate.

Jordan had suggested she call him when she came into town . . .

No! She had somehow survived three years without Jordan. Contacting him was only asking for trouble or heartbreak.

Perhaps what made her go to a phone and look up the listings of architects in the Yellow Pages was a certain recklessness, a feeling that on this marvelous day nothing could go wrong. Like a gambler, she had to make that one additional bet.

She dialed the number. The phone rang emptily. She felt relief . . . disappointment. Her jumbled thoughts froze as a male voice said crisply, "Steele and Andrews. Jordan Steele speaking."

She had been expecting to go through a receptionist or secretary. Hearing Jordan's voice without preliminaries momentarily sent her spinning. She stumbled over giving him her own name, adding, "I—I'm in town for the day, and I thought if you were free for lunch . . ." Her voice trailed off awkwardly. He hadn't *encouraged* her to call, had, in fact, agreed that it was pointless.

There was a perceptible hesitation before he said, "I thought you were coming into town last week." He made it sound as if she hadn't lived up to her word.

"I had planned to, but I decided I wanted to have more finished pieces to show. And I wanted to prepare folders displaying some of my previous work."

"I see. How did it go?" His voice was tautly neutral. She had the unexpected feeling he was stalling for time. Surely her call hadn't threatened *his* steely composure.

"Fine. I'm very encouraged. I guess I wanted someone to celebrate with me at lunch . . ."

"I'm sorry, but I already have a one o'clock lunch appointment with a client."

"Oh. I see." Barrie's soaring spirits plummeted, and even in the privacy of the phone booth she felt embarrassment and humiliation color her face. She had known she shouldn't call him. Why had she done it? Why had she given him the chance to reject her again? Like an unrealistically optimistic gambler, she had taken one too many chances on a winning streak . . . and lost. She felt vulnerably exposed and unprotected. A quick, unexpected rush of tears stung her eyes. "I—I'm sorry I bothered you, then. Goodbye."

chapter 4

"BARRIE—WAIT!"

The voice sounded peculiarly disembodied coming from the phone at arm's length from her ear. She hesitated, the receiver poised over the cradle. Slowly she returned it to her ear.

"Yes?" she said warily.

"I'm tied up for lunch, but if you plan to stay in town this afternoon, perhaps we could have dinner together." His voice sounded as wary as her own. "We could make it early, so you wouldn't be driving back to the cabin too late."

Barrie hesitated. She wanted to see him. In spite of everything, she wanted to see him. But there was a tentativeness about the invitation, almost a reluctance, as if he were half-angry at himself for making it.

"I could do some shopping." Her statement held the same lack of commitment that his wary invitation had held. She felt as if they were verbally circling, testing each other. Why should he test her, she wondered with a sudden flare of anger. It was he who had ended their previous relationship with brutal silence.

He said he'd be through at the office at five-thirty and gave her directions to the building. She said she would meet him in the parking lot. It was all very businesslike, quite impersonal.

Barrie had the addresses of two Portland firms which made opalescent glass, a type of gorgeously rich-colored glass with deep, almost iridescent swirls of color. She selected several pieces and packed them carefully in her car, then spent the remainder of the afternoon shopping at the enormous Lloyd Center shopping mall. From a viewpoint over the ice, she watched a few skaters swirl gracefully on the uncrowded, covered rink that was a surprising feature of the shopping center.

Her emotions teetered precariously between anticipation and apprehension over the coming meeting with Jordan. She thought about splurging on something dramatic and eye-catching to wear, but settled for a shimmery ice-pink scoop-necked blouse to dress up her rather utilitarian beige pants.

Uncertain of her way around Portland, she allowed plenty of time to find Jordan's building and arrived at the parking lot fifteen minutes early. She parked next to Jordan's car, putting down an adolescent urge to drive around the block until the appointed time so he wouldn't think her overeager.

She would have liked to shower and change, but she'd had to make do with freshening her makeup and changing to the new blouse in a department store's powder room. She was annoyed to find a loose thread on the blouse now and was trying to pull the thread to the underside of the material when she realized someone was standing beside the car. He was a few minutes early too.

Self-consciously she straightened the blouse. With Jordan's appraising eyes on her, the neckline suddenly felt much more revealing than it had in the store.

"Would you prefer to leave your car here or park it at my apartment?" Jordan asked. Noting the quick widening of her eyes at the mention of his apartment, he carefully elaborated. "It's just that my apartment is considerably closer than the office to the route you'll be taking home."

Again she had reacted as if she suspected him of ulterior motives, and he was carefully pointing out this was merely a dinner engagement, not an all-night invitation.

"The apartment parking lot would probably be most convenient, then. I'd like to get home early," she added coolly, to make her intentions plain also.

She followed the silver Porsche to an elegant apartment building built in a series of terraced steps up the side of one of Portland's steep hillsides. An area of the original forest vegetation of pine and fir had been preserved beside the building, giving it an air of being tucked into its surroundings. Wrought-iron balconies overlooked the city below. Jordan slid out of his car and motioned her into a visitor's parking slot.

"I thought we'd go to a restaurant across the river for dinner." He opened the door of the Porsche for her. "It shouldn't be busy at this early hour."

Barrie hesitated. This was all turning out to be so uncomfortable and awkward. Why had he asked her to dinner? He seemed less than enthusiastic over the prospect now. "I don't want to inconvenience you," she said stiffly. "Just a salad or something light would be fine."

"It isn't an inconvenience."

Neither of them made any attempt at small talk as they drove through the city and across a bridge that spanned the massive Columbia River. Mt. Hood had disappeared into a haze now. Barrie wondered if Mt. Saint Helens, the once perfect ice-cream-cone-shaped mountain that had blown its top in volcanic explosion, was visible, but Jordan was maneuvering through the heavy traffic with a scowling intensity that discouraged questions of any kind.

They parked at a motel-convention center complex on the Washington state side of the river. By now Barrie thoroughly regretted the exhilarated impulse that had prompted her to call him. He seemed to be doing this out of some grim sense of obligation. Her usual healthy appetite had vanished under a leaden weight in her stomach.

"Would you like a drink before dinner?" he inquired as they walked toward the restaurant's double doors carved with replicas of colorful Indian masks. "Or would you prefer a walk on the deck overlooking the river?"

At the moment all Barrie wanted was to get this over with as quickly as possible, but with her stomach in its present fluttery condition she doubted she could swallow either food or drink. "A walk, I guess."

He glanced at her sharply. "You don't sound very enthusiastic." He hadn't changed clothes after leaving the office, but he looked fresh and fit in the lightweight camel-tan jacket with darker pants and white shirt.

"You don't seem overjoyed yourself," she retorted.

His eyes narrowed and for a moment she thought he was simply going to march her back to the car and call off this farce. His eyes raked over her, and she had the unpleasant feeling she was being critically scrutinized from behind a closed mask, a mask she couldn't see around.

At the carved doors, he abruptly guided her to the right until they reached a wide outdoor hallway that ran between the restaurant and motel to the deck overlooking the river. In spite of her churned-up feelings inside, Barrie was entranced with the view of the wide Columbia. A couple of tugboats industriously moved barges up the river, and a ship of oceangoing size was sailing majestically downriver. There was a river scent in the air, raw but not unpleasant. Gulls wheeled and cried overhead, battling each other for prized posts on the big log pilings that held the deck against the invisible but tremendously powerful pull of the river. Barrie could hear the sound of water lapping gently at the pilings beneath the deck. Cars streamed across the bridge nearby. The scene was busy yet peaceful, and she struggled to control that uneasy churning within her.

"I appreciate your buying my stained-glass bluebird, but you didn't have to," Barrie said tentatively. "I'd have been happy to make one for you ... for your new house."

He leaned against the wooden railing. "I wouldn't expect you to do that."

"Why did you buy it?"

"It seemed just the right decoration to hang by the big window overlooking the lake. The craftsmanship is excellent. I looked at a number of stained-glass designs before buying the bedroom skylight and yours is better done than most."

"Oh." Barrie felt vaguely let down. Coming from a store owner, such praise would have been gratifying. But deep down she knew she had hoped for something more personal from Jordan. Such as what, she asked herself wryly. That he wanted a souvenir of those four passionate days they had spent together? That was unlikely, since he seemed determined to ignore the fact that those days . . . and nights . . . had existed. They were both silent as another couple holding hands strolled by. The romantic closeness of the two was in sharp contrast to the cold, formal distance between Barrie and Jordan.

"Why did you decide to come to Oregon to set up your business?" Jordan asked finally. "Why not stay back east?"

Barrie was uncertain if he really wanted to know or if he had decided to succumb to the social convention of making polite conversation. She answered in nonspecific generalities. When he made no comment, she said suddenly, "You don't think I'll stay, do you?"

His reply was succinct. "No."

"Why?"

"I think you'll go back to Killian again. I think this is just another of the little games you two play."

"Games!" Barrie repeated furiously. "You call an accident such as Killian's a *game?* I had to go back. The doctors didn't know if Killian was going to live or die after the accident. He was in the hospital for weeks."

Jordan's eyes narrowed. He half turned to look at her. The breeze lifted his thick hair, and in spite of the civilized trappings of the business suit and tie, there was a hard animal vitality to his poised stance. "I didn't know anything about an accident." His voice was wary, his look skeptical. "This was the 'emergency' you mentioned in the note you left for me?"

"Yes, of course. The other driver was killed in the accident. He was drunk. It was in the news—"

"As you may recall, I was not exactly in a position at the cabin to keep up with the latest news reports," Jordan reminded wryly.

"But I wrote you! I wrote and told you everything. You cashed my check—"

"You told me nothing!" he contradicted hotly. "You turned my life upside down and then wrote me a polite little bread-and-butter note thanking me for helping you on your vacation."

"Vacation! Why do you keep calling it a vacation?" Barrie blazed angrily. Her voice startled a seagull perched nearby and it flapped into the air with a squawk of protest. "It wasn't a vacation. We were getting a divorce."

"Vacation was your word, not mine." His coldly controlled voice matched the ice of his blue eyes.

"No! You're twisting things!" Barrie felt helpless. They seemed to have totally different views of the past, different versions of reality.

Evidently Jordan agreed on that point. "Perhaps you ought to refresh your memory," he said grimly.

"What do you mean?" Barrie faltered.

"I saved your little note. It's a helpful reminder if I should happen to forget what kind of woman you really are. And then signing the note Mrs. Killian Wright was such a cleverly discreet way of telling me where you really stood, of course. *Mrs. Killian Wright.*" He spat out the name as if it were an obscenity. "That said it all."

"I never sign my name Mrs. Killian Wright," Barrie argued angrily. Mr. and Mrs. Killian Wright on occasion, yes, of course. But after that first separation, never simply Mrs. Killian Wright, and she certainly would not have used it in writing to Jordan. "I can't understand why you're saying these things!" she added wildly.

The careful facade of politeness was gone now, and they faced each other with open hostility arcing like a current between them. The rising breeze whipped Barrie's dark hair across her face, and she brushed it back impatiently. Jordan's hands clenched the wooden railing as if he had to keep them there for control. Even the sharp blast of a tugboat horn failed to break the clashed lock of their eyes.

"Are you denying—"

"Of course I'm denying—whatever it is you're accusing me of!" Barrie looked up at him in wild defiance. "I know what I wrote you."

"Let's just see if your memory is as good as you think it is."

An elderly woman tossing scraps to the seagulls was looking at them rather oddly, her attention obviously drawn by their angry voices. Jordan smiled at the woman and put an arm around Barrie's shoulders in what to an outsider would look like a casually affectionate gesture. The woman smiled back, but Barrie could feel the relentless steel behind the imprisoning grip on her shoulders. Unless she cared to make an unpleasant scene, she had no choice but to let herself be guided back to the car. Once there, she threw off his arm with an angry gesture.

"What are you doing?" she demanded.

"I'm going to refresh your memory."

Dinner was forgotten. They recrossed the bridge. Jordan drove with machinelike speed and precision to the terraced apartment building. They took the elevator to his fourth-floor apartment. Jordan maintained a straight-lipped silence, and Barrie felt a bewildering sense of doubt. He seemed so positive . . . But she was positive too, she reminded herself. She was not about to forget how she had bared her innermost thoughts and feelings, and now to have him scathingly refer to her letter as a bread-and-butter note was too much!

He left her in the living room of the apartment with a vague wave of his hand that might or might not have been an invitation to sit down. The room was masculine, with a brushed leather sofa and massive redwood burl coffee table. The carpet was pale, creamy beige, deep and luxurious underfoot. The fireplace had antique brass andirons. Sliding glass doors opened into a small balcony bright with potted geraniums. Trees in redwood tubs screened the balcony from the view of others nearby. The view of Portland, the famed City of Roses, was breathtaking.

Jordan returned in moments. He had an envelope in one hand. He must have known exactly where to locate it. He handed it to Barrie, a glitter of triumph in his eyes.

Barrie inspected the envelope with a strange reluctance. Yes, it was her handwriting; no doubt about that. Her Washington, D. C., address was written neatly in the left-hand corner. Slowly she pulled out and unfolded the single sheet of paper the envelope held.

The note was typewritten and brief. It began with a formal "Dear Mr. Steele" and went on to thank him for his hospitality and helpful assistance during her vacation in Oregon. It asked him to take care of the rental car and mentioned an enclosed check. The closing was a typewritten, "Sincerely, Mrs. Killian Wright."

Barrie stared at the note in bewilderment, reeling under a dizzying sense of unreality. It was *there,* as real as if she had written it... but she hadn't! Her lips parted in mute, helpless protest as she tried to make sense of this. The letter had been typed on her old portable. She recognized the unmistakable lopsided *e.*

"Well?" Jordan prompted.

"I—I didn't write this." A rising note of hysteria crept into her voice as she stared at the alien words. *Hospitality.* Four nights of passion and the letter thanked him for his *hospitality.* "This isn't what I wrote at all! I explained about Killian's accident and why I had to stay with him temporarily. I told you I loved you! And then when you didn't answer—"

"How can you stand there and deny what you wrote when the proof is right there in your hand?" His voice was both incredulous and angry.

"I didn't write this," Barrie repeated doggedly. Her mind raced back over those first terrible days, when Killian lay near death in the hospital. They had let her have a room next to his, but she slept only in fitful catnaps, keeping an almost around-the-clock vigil at his bedside except when doctors or nurses gently forced her out. She had written the letter to Jordan as she sat there beside Killian, page after distraught page, with her feelings a tangle of regret and worry and guilt and responsibility and anger. She had taken the letter downstairs to mail—

No! No, she hadn't. She had given the letter to her *mother* to mail.

Slowly Barrie's gaze focused on the brief, polite type-written words again. The tone was friendly, something a polite houseguest might indeed write to weekend hosts. Barrie stared at the innocuous words with a kind of horror. Her mother had stayed at the house in Washington until Killian's life was out of danger. But surely her mother *wouldn't* have...

But she had. Mrs. Coltrane had removed the letter Barrie had written and replaced it with this caricature typed on Barrie's own typewriter, conscientiously sending along the check. *Why?* How could she? How *dare* she?

Momentarily too stunned even to feel anger at this outrage, Barrie sank to the soft leather sofa. She shook her head in helpless protest. Mrs. Coltrane must have suspected Barrie had met someone in Oregon. Then she had read Barrie's emotional letter and found out all about that passionate four-day affair with Jordan. With steely determination, she had decided to interfere and put an end to it, just as she had interfered in the filing of the divorce. The letter lay loosely in Barrie's limp hands.

Jordan scowled. "What's wrong?"

Barrie's head was still shaking in protest. "My mother . . . I can't believe it." Slowly, piecing the parts together as she went, Barrie explained what her mother had done, how she had interfered in both the divorce and this letter. In spite of her growing anger and frustration, Barrie could almost see the workings of Mrs. Coltrane's desperate mind.

Her mother had always adored Killian and, strangely enough, Killian had seemed to feel a genuine affection for her too. She had been convinced the first separation was a tragic, hasty mistake, that given a little time Barrie would "come to her senses." She had looked on the brief affair with Jordan as the unfortunate result of Barrie's misguided, confused feelings and had taken it upon herself to "protect" Barrie from her own errors in judgment. Haltingly, Barrie tried to explain all this to Jordan.

"She honestly thought she was doing the right thing. I know she thought she had my best interests at heart." Barrie had to keep telling herself that or she knew she would explode in raw fury.

She suddenly realized this explained something more: her mother's unexplained change of heart and her almost abject apologies after the second breakup. Somewhere along the line Mrs. Coltrane realized the wrong she had done, the errors she had made and compounded in her manipulations of her daughter's life. She hadn't had the courage to admit outright all that she had done, perhaps afraid she would lose Barrie completely if she did, but she obviously felt guilty and deeply remorseful.

Barrie lifted unhappy eyes to meet Jordan's. He had

dropped to the arm of the sofa as she talked. "She isn't a terrible person." Barrie shook her head, feeling helpless. There was nothing more she could do. "She isn't evil or vindictive . . ." And no wonder Jordan had been suspicious and angry, she thought. No wonder he thought their passionate affair was just a bored wife's vacation fling.

There was a long silence as Jordan's eyes searched her face. Her soul felt dissected under that probing gaze. "I want you to tell me everything," he said slowly. "From the moment you walked away through the snow that morning while I was fixing the porch until now. Everything."

Barrie told him, leaving nothing out, backtracking if she remembered any detail, no matter how minor. She told him how betrayed and lost she had felt when she heard nothing from him. She told him how she had tried to make the marriage work, but the attempt was doomed from the start. Evening shadows gathered around them in the unlighted room. The furniture made dark, bulky shapes against the pale carpet. Barrie felt drained when she had told him everything she could remember. She had momentarily relived the awful emptiness, the struggle, the decisions.

"Do you believe me?" she finally asked tremulously.

Silently he reached over and tore the letter into fluttering scraps. Then he cupped her face in his hands and looked into her eyes for a long moment before he kissed her with a lingering, almost unbearable sweetness. A warmth seeped through her, a warmth like that night long ago when she had been so cold and he had warmed her with his body. She felt as if she had been too long out in the dark cold and only now stood in the doorway of sunshine and light and warmth.

The kiss deepened as his fingers wound in the dark sable of her hair. She strained toward him, reaching, returning the deepening passion of his kiss. He stood up, never taking his lips from hers, and molded her body to the full length of his. His hands slid lower on her back and her arms wound around his neck. He lifted his head finally, and in the near darkness his face was a blur over hers. She ran her fingers through his hair and over his temples, needing to feel the hard reality of him to know this was no fantasy. She could feel his quickened breathing in the rise and fall of his chest against her breasts.

"I promised you dinner," he said huskily.

"I'm not hungry."

"I am. I've been hungry for over three years . . . wanting you . . . needing you . . ." He buried his face in the curve of her neck, and she could feel the male hunger as his body shifted to fit ever more intimately into the curves and hollows of hers.

"Oh, Jordan . . ." Her soft murmur was more a sigh than a protest against where all this was inevitably leading.

"I'm rushing things, aren't I?" he whispered contritely. "It's just that I've wanted to hold you like this again ever since that first moment I saw you looking like a scared rabbit in my kitchen."

"You didn't act as if you felt that way. I thought . . . I don't know what I thought," she confessed. "You seemed so cold and distant."

"I couldn't stay away from you. Didn't you realize that when I rushed over there the very same evening?"

"You had an excuse—"

"That's what I kept telling myself. But I'd have found some kind of excuse if I hadn't had one ready made. I watched you swimming—"

"You couldn't have seen much."

"It's surprising how much can be seen through a telescope. It doesn't have to be aimed at the mountain, you know." His voice held the husky warm laughter she remembered along with the passion.

"You didn't!" Barrie gasped indignantly. "You actually spied on me?"

"I could even see how the cold water made your breasts stand out under your bathing suit." His hand slid under the shimmery blouse and caressed the tips of her breasts into rigid peaks beneath the lacy bra. "Like that," he whispered.

"Cold water never made me feel like this." Barrie's voice was tremulous. She felt shivery and hot at the same time, as if her senses had short-circuited under the sensual electricity of his caresses.

He laughed softly and kissed her lightly on the tip of the

nose in a gently playful gesture.

"I've told you everything about the last three years of my life, and you've told me practically nothing about yours." She searched his face in the near darkness, this intimate stranger she knew so well and yet didn't really know at all.

"I'll tell you everything. Anything you want to know. Over dinner. On one condition."

"What condition?"

"That you say all night with me."

She ran her fingertips over the angular line of his jaw, savoring the texture of smooth skin over hard muscle and bone.

"I want to hold you in my arms all night. I want to love you and hold you . . ." He turned his head to catch her fingertips between his teeth in a ferocious-tender gesture.

"I don't know . . ." She wanted to stay with him. Her body was full of wild yearnings, and the circular caress of his hand over the bare skin of her back beneath the blouse was an intoxicating distraction. And yet she was afraid too, afraid the raw power of sex might plunge them too quickly into an explosive but uncertain relationship. She had to know he needed more than sex from her.

"Okay, dinner first," he compromised quickly, feeling her hesitation. He smiled and touched her lips lightly with his. "Then we'll discuss further plans."

Together they inspected Jordan's refrigerator and found enough ingredients to concoct a ham and cheese omelet. While Barrie was preparing the food in the sunny yellow kitchen, Jordan disappeared and shortly returned with a bottle of champagne. He said the occasion demanded no less and poured the pale, bubbly liquid into long-stemmed glasses. He took off his jacket and turned back the cuffs of his white shirt, and she slipped out of her high-heeled sandals.

They ate and drank, and Jordan kept her laughing with amusing stories of his first experience designing solar homes in the Portland area. The laughter and heady effects of the champagne combined to make Barrie feel relaxed and happy as they wandered out to the balcony, champagne glasses still in hand. Jordan paused along the way to switch on the stereo, and a flowing wave of soft guitar music followed them. They stood at the iron railing, looking down at the lights of the city. Late-evening light still lingered in the summer sky, and only a handful of stars glimmered off to the east. They stood with shoulders touching companionably.

"When I didn't come to town and call you last week, you took it as another indication of my—unreliability, didn't you?"

"Something like that," he admitted.

"You didn't sound as if you particularly wanted me to call," she chided gently.

"Can you blame me? I thought . . . well, you know what I thought."

"And it was just as wrong as what I thought." She hesitated. "I have to keep reminding myself that my mother really believed she was doing what was best."

He didn't say anything, but there was no animosity in the silence. Overhead, beyond sound, a jet silently stretched a shimmering ribbon across the sky. They watched the narrow line slowly widen, like a path across the sky for unseen gods of the night.

"When do you plan to move out to the lake?" Barrie asked. She spoke with a kind of idle, dreamy curiosity.

"In a few weeks. I'm not certain exactly when yet."

"Will you miss all this?" She lifted her champagne glass in a little wave that took in both the magnificent view and city life in general.

"I'm looking forward to a . . . ah . . . close association with my new neighbors at the lake." He turned to face her and clasped his hands together at the back of her waist in a loose embrace as he smiled down at her.

She leaned back to look up into his face, feeling a little giddy from the champagne and yet secure within the protective circle of his arms. She could feel the hard, sinewy muscles of his braced legs. She swallowed the last sip of champagne and leaned over to set the glass on the low patio table. Her breast brushed his arm in comfortable intimacy. She studied his strong face. They had kept dinner light and yet there were things that must be said.

"I—I feel that the slate has been wiped clean. That we have a chance to start all over again." It was a statement and yet there was a tentativeness about the words that made them a question too.

His eyes searched her face. "Do you want to start all over again?"

"Do you?" she parried.

"What do you think?"

The loose embrace tightened as he pulled her to him, and his mouth found hers as if it were coming home. Barrie returned the kiss, losing herself in it, drifting dreamily, feeling as if she were spinning weightlessly along that path in the night sky.

She made only the faintest murmur of protest, no more than a sigh, when he swept her up in his arms and carried her through the dim living room to the dark bedroom. He set her gently on the bed, and then the bed sagged slightly as his heavier weight stretched out beside her.

He lay on his side, head supported by one hand while the other hand softly explored her face and throat. "I want to touch you," he said softly. "I want to know you all over again the way I once did." His hand slid over her breast, the small gesture emphasizing the barrier of fabric.

She skimmed out of the blouse, feeling a small, shaky ripple of laughter mixed with the diffused excitement of awakening passion. Had she chosen the blouse with an eye to its ease of removal in mind?

"Why are you laughing?"

She told him. He laughed too, and then the laughter ceased as the bra slipped away beneath his deft hands. She felt more than heard the low growl of pleasure deep in his throat as his hand freely roamed the soft curves of her naked skin. Against her bare back the velvet spread felt sensuously luxurious, but it was no match for the heady pleasure of his caressing hand. His mouth found first one breast and then the other as his hand slid down to explore the curve of her hip and the flat plane of her abdomen.

Her hands tangled in his thick hair. Her eyes were closed, her head arched back against the pillow as her body moved in rhythm with the caress of his hand. It was not a light touch. The slow caress had a depth, a pressure. She could feel some inner part of her that had long been cold and inert growing warmer... smoldering... glowing... hovering on the edge of a liquid melting.

With an uncharacteristic tremor, his hand groped for the zipper on her slacks. Barrie's hand covered his, stopping him. It was an instinctive more than a deliberate gesture.

"Barrie..." he protested hoarsely. His hand found the tab on the zipper and moved it downward an inch before her touch stopped him again.

It was foolish, she thought wildly. She was half-naked. She could feel the pulsing throb of his male desire, and there was an empty ache inside her that demanded fulfillment. His head lifted from her breasts and rested lightly against her cheek. She could feel the damp sheen of perspiration on his forehead.

"I'm doing this all wrong, aren't I?" he asked ruefully. "Groping and pawing at you like some overeager adolescent."

"Plying me with champagne," she agreed softly. "Seducing me with romantic music."

"Stay with me," he whispered. "I want to make love to you with all the time in the world. And wake up with you in my arms."

A night in Jordan's arms. . . . The prospect was a magic carpet stretched out temptingly before her, a pathway from delights remembered to ecstasies to come.

"You want to stay. I know you do."

Yes. She had the wild, soaring feeling that she could crawl into bed with Jordan and not come out for days. And she didn't need the excuse of a snowstorm.

"Sex is such a... a powerful force," she said haltingly. "Powerful and important... and sometimes misleading..."

He slid over her and she could feel the probe of his eyes even in the darkness. "Do you think I'm misleading you?"

His weight over her felt solid and dependable, heavy but not crushing. "No. But I feel as if we're moving too fast. The way we did before."

"Maybe we need to move fast," he murmured. His lips

nibbled her ear in a gently teasing gesture. "We have a lot of lost time to make up for."

"I feel as if we're perhaps skipping something important..." Her voice trailed off because she wasn't sure just what it was she was trying to put into words. She only knew that this meant so much to her that she wanted to be sure nothing went wrong.

"Such as what?" He sounded honestly perplexed. "What are we skipping?"

"I don't know...getting to know each other?" She swallowed. "Maybe it's all just sex between us. And sex alone isn't enough for forever..."

She felt a flush tinge her cheeks in the darkness. Now it was she who was rushing. He had said nothing about *forever*. Just tonight. "I don't mean—" she began helplessly.

He touched a silencing finger to her lips. "I know what you mean."

He didn't move but she could feel the thoughts moving in his mind, balancing and weighing what she was saying against the desire that throbbed with a physical ache between them. For a moment his body drove hard, almost painfully against hers, trapping the breath in her chest and crushing her pelvis against the bed. Then, with a spasmodic movement in his throat, he relaxed.

"I guess forever is worth waiting for," he said huskily. His lips touched hers lightly. "But don't go yet. I want to hold you just a little longer. But not like this."

Impatiently he ripped off his shirt. Then slowly, as if savoring the sensuous pleasure, he lowered his body until his naked chest touched her yielding breasts with no barrier between them. They lay together a long time, talking and laughing softly. The volatile chemistry was still there between them but carefully held to a controlled simmer. When Barrie finally left the apartment, Jordan promised he'd see her sometime Saturday, after he finished with an early client.

Barrie drove home feeling exhilarated and exultant, riding high on a wave of happiness and anticipation. They had made a fresh start. The tangled past was behind them. The love she had long denied was free to come out of the shadows of doubt and suspicion, to grow and bloom.

And the thought that the higher she flew the farther she had to fall was only a fleeting and instantaneously dismissed shadow on her joy.

chapter 5

THE NEXT DAY was one of those rare, marvelous times when it seemed as if nothing could go wrong. Mike Setlow showed up early and efficiently set about bracing the carport to its original position. Barrie's own work flowed smoothly. Her glass cuts broke precisely, with no dismaying cracks running off at strange angles. The lead came was cooperatively pliable and flexible. She managed to outsmart the eccentric electrical system and didn't blow a single fuse all day while using her soldering iron.

The phone company showed up with a machine that dug a narrow, deep trench from the main phone line to her cabin. The workmen laid a snaky-looking cable at the bottom of the trench and told her she should have a phone by the next day. And underneath it all, like lilting background music, danced her happy thoughts about Jordan.

Mike wanted to continue working in the cool of the evening, so Barrie fixed hamburgers for supper for both of them. By the time he left that evening, he had the outside repairs finished and was ready to start on inside work.

The next day was almost as satisfactory. But not quite.

Barrie's work went nicely. She'd have no trouble filling the order for the Mt. Hood window hangings on time. The telephone company workmen returned and installed her phone. In the heat of the afternoon, she decided to take a break for a cooling swim. Mike stripped out of his T-shirt and boots and joined her in his jeans. He was a competent swimmer but no match for Barrie's lithe agility and speed.

"Haven't you ever heard a girl isn't supposed to outdo a guy like that?" he grumbled cheerfully as he crawled up on a large flat rock beside her after she had outdistanced him in a short sprint. "Shatters his male ego."

"I'm no girl," Barrie retorted tartly. "I'm a twenty-seven-year-old divorcee. Remember?"

"Remarkably well preserved, however." He let his eyes drift lazily over her trimly curvaceous figure. His voice was light but Barrie felt a sudden instinctive warning that she had better be on guard, that Mike might easily get amorous ideas that would make for an awkward and unwanted situation. She suspected he already had a few ideas as his gaze lingered on the low-cut top of her swimsuit, and she remembered Jordan's comments about the cold water's effect on her breasts.

She stretched out on her stomach on the warm, flat rock, head cradled on her crossed arms. "Do you have another job after you finish up here?" she asked, to change the subject.

"Maybe another day or two at that new house across the lake." He motioned in the direction of Jordan's home. "It's quite a place. Did you go through it when they had the open house?"

"Yes. It was very interesting," Barrie said noncommittally. "You helped build it?"

"Just a day or two now and then when one of the regular carpenters was sick or something." He was too modest or honest to enlarge his part. "An architect owns it."

"I imagine he intends to use it as a model or showcase for his work," Barrie murmured. The exertion of swimming and the soothing warmth of the rock were making her feel pleasantly drowsy.

Mike's next words jolted her instantly awake.

"I think he has other plans. I doubt if he's been bringing that blonde out here all summer just to ask her advice about the interior decorating."

"Blonde?" Barrie echoed. The way Mike used the word

blonde conveyed more than hair color. There was a definite sexiness implied.

"I guess she's an interior decorator. At least that's what the sign on the van she drives says. Though she really looks too young."

"How young?"

"Maybe eighteen or nineteen."

"Eighteen or nineteen!" Barrie jerked to a sitting position, eyes riveted on Mike in surprise. In the candid discussion of their three-year separation, Jordan had obviously left out a few details. She was suddenly aware that Mike was regarding her curiously, no doubt surprised by her agitated reaction to what to him was just a bit of idle gossip. She stretched out on her back on the rock, shielding her eyes from the sun with one arm. "There must be a considerable difference in their ages." With resolute self-control, she kept her voice to an idly conversational tone. Jordan, she calculated swiftly, must be at least thirty-four now.

"Yeah. Steele's pretty smooth."

Barrie was uncertain whether the brief comment was critical or envious. "Perhaps she's a relative. A niece or something." She realized she was casting around for a suitable explanation more for her own benefit than Mike's.

"I don't think so." Both Mike's words and his little knowing chuckle said he had good reason to believe there was more than an uncle-niece relationship between Jordan and his young blonde.

The flat rock suddenly felt uncomfortably hot and hard against Barrie's back. She didn't want to hear more about this subject, but she had to fight down a perverse temptation to pry details out of Mike. She jumped to her feet and dove crisply off the sharp edge of the rock overhanging the lake.

The cold water was a shock to her sun-warmed skin, but it also jolted her mind out of that first absurd and rather childish reaction. Jordan was, after all, an extremely attractive man and virilely male. She would hardly expect that he had spent the last three years without the pleasure of female companionship. Jordan had evidently not felt it necessary to mention the girl, so their relationship must not be too serious or permanent.

With that thought held firmly in hand, Barrie managed to get through the night and next morning with a fair degree of equaniinity. She worked industriously. She had three of the Mt. Hood pieces almost finished now, needing only the application of a liquid patina to take away the lead came's shiny look and give it a mellow antique finish.

Barrie dutifully called her mother to let her know the telephone had been installed, and they had a pleasant chat. She hadn't yet reached the point where she could totally forgive what her mother had done, so she kept silent on the sensitive subject in spite of her mother's careful but rather transparent questions asking if she had made new friends or run into anyone she had known before at the lake.

She kept reminding herself that when she saw Jordan she must not ask curious questions, or even make hints about the girl. She must simply trust him.

Barrie more or less expected Jordan by lunchtime on Saturday, but by late afternoon he still had not arrived. Trying not to feel disappointed or apprehensive, she took her usual late afternoon swim.

Floating on her back, she watched with only idle interest as a small boat headed in her direction from the far side of the lake. The lake had a low speed limit, holding boats to trolling speeds, so the boat's progress was not rapid. It was halfway across the lake before Barrie realized the lone occupant was waving.

Jordan! Barrie swam out to meet the boat, her vague apprehension vanished in giddy bubbles of happiness. She swam alongside the boat and Jordan helped her in. Trailing rivulets of water on his chest, she leaned over to plant a warm, wet welcoming kiss on his mouth.

"This is marvelous!" she said delightedly. "I didn't know you had a boat."

The small fiberglass boat was squeaky new and clean, and the little outboard engine, equally new, purred smoothly.

"I just bought it a few days ago and they delivered it today."

"Do you like to fish?" It was another of the many small details she didn't know about him.

"So far I've been too busy, but I plan to give it a try."

Barrie tilted her head over the edge of the boat, squeezed the water out of her dark hair, then slicked it back from her face. Water dripped off her body and formed a warm puddle around her on the padded seat. She chattered about the work she'd finished and the repairs on the cabin. They were almost to the shore before she realized she was doing most of the talking and Jordan wasn't saying much. He wasn't exactly withdrawn, but there was a certain reserve about him that she found disquieting. They had parted on such close, wonderful terms Wednesday night that she was puzzled. What had happened?

Her own words about sex being a powerful but sometimes misleading force suddenly rushed back to her. Did he feel differently about her in the bright light of day than he had in the darkness with his mind blurred with sexual desire? Had he started comparing her unfavorably with his nineteen-year-old blonde?

Jordan cut the engine and let the small boat glide into a natural vee between two rocks. Barrie jumped out and tied the rope to a young pine. Jordan climbed out behind her. He was wearing faded jeans and an old tank top. He looked hard and ruggedly muscular. She also had the quick impression that he was carefully avoiding touching her. Well, that was probably sensible, she rationalized. She was the one who had said they shouldn't rush things, and touching with them had always started incendiary feelings that were practically impossible to shut off. Jordan's detached expression looked anything but incendiary right now, however.

"I bought a couple of steaks. I thought we could barbecue them outside," Barrie suggested tentatively as they started toward the cabin. "I was expecting you earlier."

"Sounds fine." He didn't explain the delay.

Barrie already had the small cast-iron grill set up behind the cabin. Jordan expertly started the charcoal briquets burning. Barrie had salad crisping in the refrigerator. She hadn't any liquor on hand, but she had made sun tea, setting tea bags in a big jar of water in the sun until the natural heat produced tea. She dumped ice cubes into two glasses and filled them with the tea. She carried the glasses back outside and handed one to Jordan, trying to work up her nerve to ask him if something was wrong. He hadn't clearly indicated anything *was* wrong actually, but neither did things seem quite right.

She sat on the back steps, her arms clasped around her knees. "Everything go all right with your client this morning?" she asked tentatively, her eyes on the gray ash forming on the edges of the charcoal briquets. There was a warm pine scent in the air and the faint put-put of a fisherman's boat trolling on the lake. The mountain was a benevolent presence beyond the forested foothills. It was all very peaceful and Jordan looked quite domestic tending the barbecue grill, but Barrie sensed less tranquil undercurrents.

"Client?" He sounded absentminded. "Oh yes, everything went fine. I was also telling a friend of mine about your work with stained glass, and she's interested in meeting you. I think she could be very helpful in introducing you to potential customers and perhaps using your creations in her own work."

"How nice!" Barrie felt a quick rush of warmth and gratitude. Perhaps she had only imagined Jordan's cool aloofness. His helpful attitude toward her work was so much different from Killian's disdain. "Who is she?"

"Her name is Vanessa Thompson. She's an interior decorator."

Barrie clutched the damp glass to keep from dropping it. He wanted her to *meet* his young blond playmate? "Don't you think that could be a little awkward?" she asked, astonished at the casualness with which he made the suggestion.

"I don't see why." He scowled slightly.

The unexpected honk of a horn sounded from the front of the cabin. Barrie excused herself, glad of the momentary chance to escape as her thoughts whirled erratically. She rounded the corner of the house and practically bumped into Mike Setlow, heading for the front door. She had slipped jeans on over her swimsuit and Mike's roving eyes appreciated the combination. He was dressed in neat slacks and knit shirt.

"Hey, I just decided kind of on the spur of the moment

to drive up to Timberline Lodge this evening. Would you like to come along?"

Barrie felt a possessive hand on her hip at the same moment she saw the surprised widening of Mike's blue eyes. Jordan had followed her around the cabin.

"I didn't know you had company." Mike glanced around surreptitiously, as if wondering how Jordan had materialized so suddenly. There was no extra car in sight, of course, and the small boat was hidden by the rocks. "I guess I should have called," he added lamely.

"Barrie is busy this evening." Jordan stood beside her, his arm around her with a hand openly resting on her hip in the aggressive manner of one male animal giving a warning signal to another that he is invading territorial limits.

"Yeah. Well, sure." Mike looked more surprised than unhappy at finding Jordan at the cabin, but out of the corner of her eye Barrie could see the faint lines of a scowl on Jordan's face. "See you Monday then," Mike said as he headed back toward his old pickup.

"Mike is the carpenter who is doing the repairs on the cabin," Barrie explained as Mike rattled off in the pickup.

"That doesn't sound like all he's doing." Jordan's voice was caustically insinuating, but his hand lingered on her hip, the strong fingers cupping the curve in an intimate way that sent a suggestive tingle through Barrie's body.

She looked up into the brooding smolder of his blue eyes, and for a moment was recklessly tempted to press her body against his in a brazen diversionary tactic to get him out of this mood. Perhaps sensing her thoughts, he abruptly released her and stepped back, his expression suddenly distant. The deliberate rejection hit Barrie like a dash of ice water. Jordan obviously intended to hold any physical feelings in check tonight.

Which was what she wanted . . . so why was she feeling so rejected, she wondered disconsolately.

"Yes, Mike is building storage bins for my stained glass too," Barrie finally said, though she knew full well that wasn't what Jordan had meant with his caustic comment. She was puzzled and a little annoyed at Jordan's reaction to Mike's unexpected visit. Of course she was busy this evening and would have told Mike so, but she felt she should have been the one to say that, not Jordan.

They returned to the barbecue grill. The charcoal was just at the right stage of heat, and Jordan arranged the steaks on the metal grill. "If you'd like to see Timberline Lodge, we can drive up there sometime." He paused momentarily, then added almost challengingly, "Next Saturday?"

Barrie nodded. She had never been up to the famous lodge on Mt. Hood. "Fine. I've heard the lodge has a basement bar called the Blue Ox with some interesting stained-glass murals showing Paul Bunyan and his blue ox."

The sizzling steaks scented the early evening air with a tantalizing aroma. Barrie busied herself carrying out plates and silverware and other food she had prepared.

"Have you been dating Mike?" Jordan finally asked casually.

Almost too casually, Barrie thought. She set aluminum foil-wrapped packets of French bread on the grill to warm. "No, he's just working for me." Then, for total honesty's sake, she amended the statement slightly. "We did go out for pizza together one evening. And I fixed hamburgers here once so he could stay and work in the evening."

"I see."

The inflection in those two words said to Barrie that Jordan "saw" considerably more than there really was to see, but it was his next words that really sent a jolt of incredulous shock through her.

"Don't you think he's a little young for you?"

Barrie's hand stopped in midair as she was refilling the iced tea glasses. She glanced at Jordan who was almost savagely spearing and flipping the steaks. She had no romantic interest in Mike Setlow, but if she had, what difference should it make if he were a few years younger? And considering the age circumstance's of *Jordan's* involvement . . .

"I'm under the impression there is considerably less difference between my age and Mike's than there is between the ages of you and your interior decorator." Barrie's statement was coolly deliberate, but there was a tremor in her hand as she returned to filling the iced tea glasses.

Jordan stood up, his full height intimidating from her kneeling position. "What's that supposed to mean?"

"Just what the words said. I think they were plain enough." How dare he sound so self-righteous!

"Vanessa Thompson is in her mid-fifties. I suppose that qualifies as a considerable age difference, but I'm afraid the significance escapes me. She's widowed, with two children and half a dozen grandchildren."

"But I heard—" Barrie broke off, aware she had been caught listening to gossip and bewildered by this contradictory information about the interior decorator.

"You heard what?" Jordan prodded.

"I heard you'd been bringing an eighteen- or nineteen-year-old girl out to the lake all summer." Barrie felt flustered by her obvious error about Jordan's relationship with the interior decorator. Defensively she added, "She drives a van with something about an interior decorator printed on the side."

With careful deliberation Jordan checked the steaks and then transferred them to the plates Barrie had waiting. "She's Vanessa's niece and is working for her this summer. She has driven Vanessa's van over here a few times."

"I see." Barrie couldn't keep a sarcastic note out of her voice as she added, *"She* has a name, I presume."

"Tricia Dorset."

"How old is she?" Barrie demanded bluntly.

"Nineteen, I believe." He hesitated only slightly before adding, "She'll start her sophomore year at Oregon State this fall."

A *college* girl. "You seem to have something of a double standard," Barrie snapped. "A college girl half your age is fine for you, but a college guy three years my junior is a 'little young' for me."

For that matter, there was a greater difference between her own and Jordan's ages than between hers and Mike's. Jordan definitely operated on a double standard, she thought angrily.

"Tricia is somewhat more than *half* my age," Jordan said dryly. "Unless I've missed counting a few birthdays."

"Why didn't you tell me about this girl?" Barrie demanded, hurt mixed with anger. "I told you *everything*."

"It didn't seem important." He thrust a plate at her. "How did you happen to hear about her?"

"I don't think *that* is important."

But of course they both knew Mike had told her. She waited for Jordan to say something more, explain about the girl, *something*, but he didn't.

"Your steak is getting cold," he said flatly, eyeing the plate she was clutching with both hands.

The subject was obviously closed as far as Jordan was concerned. His face had a closed, remote look too. Barrie suspected he might have liked to ask a few more questions about her relationship with Mike, but not asking was a trade off to avoid some deeper discussion of the girl.

Some disinterested part of her noted that the meat was juicy and delicious, the salad crisp, the French bread buttery warm, but she ate with no more enjoyment than if it were all sawdust. Finally she took a deep breath. She couldn't let this happen.

"Jordan, this is ridiculous. Mike is just a nice kid. And I didn't expect that you'd never looked at another girl during the last three—"

The jarring shrill of the phone made Barrie jump. It was the first time the phone had rung since being installed.

"Excuse me," she said stiffly. Her attempt to resolve what was really a minor and foolish matter had so far made no impact on Jordan's withdrawn expression.

Inside the cabin, Barrie jerked the phone to her ear. Through a window she could see Jordan at the picnic table. His back looked rigidly uncompromising. Her "Hello" came out an unfriendly snap.

"I've been trying to reach you," Killian said without preliminaries. He sounded impatient and annoyed at her for not being instantly available when he wanted her. The same old Killian, she thought wryly.

"The phone was installed only yesterday."

"I see."

The implication, of course, was that if she'd been on her toes the phone would have been installed when he wanted to reach her. After the go-round with Jordan only moments earlier, Barrie was in no mood to cater to Killian's arrogance. "What do you want?" she demanded bluntly.

There was a problem with some insurance papers. Killian explained at some length what seemed to Barrie to be an inconsequential matter that could have been solved simply by sending the papers to her for her signature. He finally said that was what he would do.

"And how are you getting along?" he asked. There was a change in his voice and she realized in surprise that he was trying to convey a personal interest and concern rather than merely asking the conventionally meaningless question. "It's good to hear your voice." He paused for emphasis. "Washington can be a very lonely place."

Oh no, Barrie thought grimly. She wasn't going to let him lay some guilt and responsibility thing on her. Was Killian getting some backlash from the older representative he had replaced, a man who was practically a fanatic against divorce and still wielded tremendous political power in the state? She resisted an urge to make some caustic comment about his other women taking care of his loneliness.

"I'm just fine, thank you," she said briskly. "I have some company waiting, so if that's everything—?"

She could feel his unspoken question. What kind of company?

"Certainly." He sounded stiff and a little angry. "Nice talking to you."

Barrie went back outside. Her half-eaten steak was cold, and the juice had congealed into a greasy puddle. She determinedly attacked the meat anyway, but in her nervous hands the steak knife slipped and skittered across the picnic table.

Jordan returned the knife. "That was your husband on the phone, wasn't it?"

"He is *not* my husband!" How had Jordan known who the caller was?

Jordan ignored the protest. "Is he trying to get you to come back to him?"

Was he? Barrie's momentary hesitation was evidently enough to lend credence to Jordan's suspicion even though

Barrie said firmly, "No, he did not ask me to come back to him. He called about a business matter. Some insurance papers."

"What if he had asked?"

Barrie pushed the plate aside, unable to eat any more. "You feel differently about me than you did the other night, don't you?" she asked squarely. "I've felt it ever since you stepped off the boat."

"I suppose there are a few unresolved questions in my mind," he agreed coolly. He was gazing off into space, a slight frown on his face.

And Mike's appearance and Killian's phone call hadn't helped matters any, Barrie thought unhappily. The timing couldn't have been worse. She had a strawberry and ice cream dessert waiting in the refrigerator, but she didn't go through the polite gesture of offering it. Neither of them was in a mood for dessert. "Then let's hear your questions," she said determinedly.

"I've spent a few spare moments wondering why the divorce papers show Killian divorced you instead of the other way around." He paused, his eyes roaming her face reflectively. "Perhaps you didn't even want the divorce."

Unemotionally, Barrie explained that the divorce was her idea but she assumed Killian saw political advantages to his filing. "I think he was afraid if I filed that I'd bring up his extramarital involvements," she added.

"And you weren't afraid he'd bring up yours?"

Barrie met the open challenge directly. "There weren't any. Except you. And he never knew about you."

He pounced on her statement. "But you did consider me extramarital."

"No!" Barrie protested. Flustered, she amended that. "Technically, I suppose so, under the circumstances . . ."

Jordan let her flounder before deliberately attacking her from another direction with another question. "What if Killian does decide he wants you back?"

That was a question Barrie could answer without qualifications. "I wouldn't go back under any circumstances."

"You went back once."

"That was different. He was hurt, perhaps even dying—"

"He could get hurt again," Jordan persisted relentlessly. "Or need you desperately for some other reason. I take it he hasn't remarried?"

"No. I presume he thought too quick a remarriage would look suspicious and be inadvisable politically." Barrie's temper was rising under this barrage of biting questions and suspicions, and she launched a counterattack of her own. "You seem to find something deep and meaningful in the fact that Killian divorced me instead of the other way around, as if this proves I'd jump at the chance to go back to him."

Jordan's cocked eyebrow registered a what-are-you-getting-at wariness. He leaned his elbows on the weathered table and folded his arms.

"You were married before. Who divorced whom?"

"She divorced me."

"And will you go running back if she asks you to?"

"It's an entirely different situation." He dismissed the subject of his own marriage as if it were totally irrelevant. "She's remarried and has four children." And then he was on the attack again, persistent as some ruthless predator following a fresh trail. "You say you went back to Killian out of a sense of duty and responsiblity. Somehow it's hard to believe that a sense of duty kept you there *three years*. Killian was back on his feet in a few months, wasn't he?"

Barrie stared at Jordan with her feelings a tangle of anger, dismay, and bewilderment. She had tried to explain all this to him the other night, but evidently those explanations had not satisifed him. At least not after he was out of bed with her, she thought grimly, and had something other than sex on his mind.

She stood up and started snatching haphazardly at plates and silverware and glasses. Jordan's hand closed over her wrist.

"I take it you prefer not to discuss this further?" His voice was as harsh as the grip on her wrist.

"Discuss? *Discuss?*" she repeated wildly. "You don't

want to discuss anything. You're deliberately trying to pick an argument with me! First over Mike, and when that back-fired because of your own—"

The sudden narrowing of his eyes told her that barb had jabbed home.

"When that backfired," she repeated defiantly, "you de-cided to pick an argument about Killian. Are you afraid if we don't fight that I'll demand some lifetime commitment just because you said a few things you didn't mean when you were trying to persuade me to have sex with you?"

She deliberately did not call the act making love, delib-erately used the more crude and less personal term. Strangers could have sex. It took something more to make love. And right now she felt as if Jordan were a total stranger.

"I don't say things I don't mean," Jordan growled.

"But sometimes you have second thoughts." Barrie's hand felt bloodless with his harsh grip constricting her wrist. "Now if you'll excuse me, I have work to do."

He released her wrist with a certain reluctance. "I should get the boat back across the lake before dark."

If he thought she was going to try to persuade him dif-ferently, he was mistaken. She merely nodded tightly and went on cleaning up the dinner things. She dumped the melted ice from her glass on the barbecue grill. The doused briquets gave off a dismal sizzle of steam and a sodden, burned odor.

That was the way the evening had ended, Barrie thought unhappily as she watched Jordan head toward the boat with-out looking back. Dismal and sodden. And as dead and cold as the wet charcoal.

Was he jealous, Barrie wondered. No. The doubts and suspicions had been working on his mind before he ever came here today, and the unfortunate encounter with Mike and phone call from Killian had merely served to confirm his distrustful suspicions. Even after all she had told him, he still stubbornly believed she'd run back to Killian if he wanted her. Or was that just some kind of smokescreen to put her on the defensive and free him to chase his blond playmate? And she had been so determined to be broad-minded about his college-age girl friend, she mused bitterly.

The next day she saw Jordan fishing from his boat. He wasn't working very hard at it. The boat drifted idly while he lay back with a straw hat over his face. Barrie watched him from the concealment of a kitchen window and felt totally frustrated by the previous day's events. Had Jordan been miffed because she had refused to spend the night at his apartment? No, she couldn't believe he was that shallow.

Perhaps her argument about the possible deceptiveness of sexual attraction had been too convincing, she thought ruefully. She had seen the quick smolder of desire in his eyes, and just as quickly he had backed off, as if wary of what might happen. She was debating with herself about swimming out to the boat when the honk of a horn made him sit up and look toward shore. He immediately started reeling in his fishing line.

A van had just parked in his driveway, and a girl was standing beside it. Barrie was too far away to read the printing on the side of the van, but she had no doubt what it said. And she didn't need a telescope such as Jordan had used to spy on her to know that the girl who stood beside the van was very blond. And very young.

chapter 6

THE VAN WAS still in Jordan's driveway by the time dusk
blurred Barrie's view across the lake, but it was gone when
she rushed to the window first thing next morning to check.
Which didn't necessarily prove anything, she thought unhappily.

Mike showed up right after breakfast and started work
on her storage bins. He didn't ask any outright questions
about her relationship with Jordan, but he kept giving her
little sideways, curious glances. His attitude toward her also
seemed to have changed. He didn't kid around as much or
make his cheerfully suggestive little remarks about her figure or her living alone or the difference in their ages. It was
as if he were tacitly acknowledging Jordan had established
some sort of property rights to her, rights he wouldn't consider violating.

The situation left Barrie silently fuming at both men—
at Jordan for his chauvinistic attitude about age differences,
and not listening to her explanation about Killian's call; at
Mike for calmly accepting Jordan's warning signals . . .

She threw herself into her work and by Thursday, she
had the order for Mt. Hood pieces ready, plus several more
samples to show. On Thursday evening, she received a
telephone call from Jordan. He was coolly businesslike. He
had arranged a luncheon meeting for her with Vanessa
Thompson the following day, if Barrie could make it. Just

as businesslike, she said she could. He named a time and restaurant and gave her efficient directions.

Would he be at the lunch too? He didn't say, and stubbornly she refused to ask, too proud to let him think his presence mattered one way or the other to her.

The restaurant was a restored Victorian house complete with elaborately railed porch, gingerbread curlicues, and a peaked tower. Above the entry door was a family crest beautifully done in stained glass. Inside, Barrie gave her name and was led down a high-ceilinged hallway to one of the intimate dining rooms.

Jordan was just seating a woman at the table. His presence, half-hoped for, half-dreaded, sent a shivery little shock through Barrie. The woman was middle-aged but elegant looking in a tanned, outdoor way. She had silver-blond hair and a husky, good-natured laugh as she said something over her shoulder to Jordan. Barrie was surprised to see Jordan remove a wooden crutch she had been using and lean it against the delicately-patterned wallpapered wall. She was even more surprised, and considerably more dismayed, to see a third person at the table. The girl had sun-kissed blond hair, loose and windswept, a sprinkling of freckles across a pert nose, and a youthful, glowing vitality.

Barrie didn't need an introduction to know this was Tricia Dorset. She was wearing a full, print skirt paired with a cotton blouse in a different print, but on her the combination looked youthfully carefree rather than mismatched. Barrie suddenly felt almost too carefully put together in her matching champagne-beige slacks and blazer.

Determinedly swallowing her sudden consternation, Barrie put a smile on her face. "Hello! I hope I'm not late."

The older woman smiled. "Of course not. Right on time."

Jordan made the introductions. He introduced Tricia as if no mention of her had ever before passed between Barrie and himself.

"I clumsily managed to break my leg." Vanessa nodded toward the crutch leaning against the wall. "So my niece Tricia has been my chauffeur and general all-around 'gofer' while she's on vacation from college this summer. I'm finally out of the cast, but I still need that crutch."

"A broken leg must be very inconvenient," Barrie murmured. She was aware of Tricia openly studying her. "How did it happen?"

"Vanity." Vanessa laughed at herself. "Pure vanity. I stepped back to admire the marvelous effect I'd just created in a loft bedroom and tumbled right down the stairs."

Barrie liked Vanessa Thompson immediately. She had shrewd but friendly blue eyes, and her husky chuckle was infectious.

The waitress took their orders. While they waited for their lunch to be served, Vanessa questioned Barrie about what type of stained-glass work she had done, what techniques and types of materials she used. Her questions were friendly but knowledgeable. She nodded approvingly when Barrie said that except for the special opalescent glass she had purchased here in Portland, she used only mouth-blown, usually German, glass. Barrie brought out one of her display folders and, after penning in her new phone number, gave it to Vanessa.

Tricia did not enter into the conversation, but Barrie was very much aware of the younger girl's presence. A word popped into her head as salads arrived and she had an opportunity to snatch a few covert glances at Tricia. *Virginal.* Tricia exuded a certain sexiness with her tousled hair and wide eyes, but it was a virginal sexiness, as if she were innocent of its effect. Was she, Barrie wondered with a certain skepticism as out of the corner of her eye she saw Tricia deliberately brush her shoulder against Jordan's as she leaned toward him.

Had Jordan known Tricia would be present at the lunch? If he was uncomfortable with Barrie sitting on one side of him and Tricia on the other, he had far too much self-control to give the slightest indication of it. The thought also occurred to Barrie that perhaps Jordan had purposely wanted Tricia's presence here today to send a silent message to Barrie. A message to remind her she had no claims on him just because they shared a certain volatile sexual attraction.

"Are you planning to be an interior decorator too?" Barrie asked Tricia during a lull in the conversation. Except for acknowledging Jordan's introductions, they had not yet spoken directly to each other.

"Oh no! I couldn't stand to be inside so much. I prefer the outdoors," Tricia laughed. She had a flash of healthy white teeth, but her laugh lacked her aunt's good-humored warmth.

"What are you studying at college?"

"So far I'm sampling a bit of everything. I'm fascinated by archaeology—"

"And astronomy," Vanessa added.

"And agriculture," Jordan put in. "That takes care of the *a*'s. Now under *b* there's biology, bacteria—"

Barrie joined in the laughter. Jordan and Vanessa were obviously indulgently amused and tolerant of Tricia's youthful experimentation. A bit less generous, Barrie thought it might also reflect a certain flightiness and immature inability to stick to anything difficult.

After lunch, they all went out to Barrie's car. She unpacked one of the Mt. Hood pieces to show Vanessa, plus the other samples she had created. One was a lake scene with trees in the background.

"Oh, this one is marvelous!" Vanessa exclaimed. "Is it spoken for?"

"But it has so many flaws," Tricia objected suddenly. "Look at all the imperfections in the blue glass."

Barrie's lips parted in surprise. The comment was obviously meant to downgrade the quality of her work. Keeping her anger under control, Barrie carefully explained that high-quality mouth-blown glass had small air pockets or bubbles trapped at the time the glass was originally blown. These were called seeds and were highly prized. They gave each sheet of glass a unique character. "I made a special effort to cut the glass so as to include as many seeds as possible," she said evenly. "I've heard them described as trapped sunlight."

"Yes . . . see how the bubbles emphasize the water effect in the lake?" Vanessa agreed, running a slim finger over the blue glass.

"Oh."

Tricia's expression was sullen. Barrie's careful comments had made Tricia's criticism look foolish, and Tricia was obviously annoyed with that outcome. She moved over closer to Jordan and slipped a hand around his arm. Jordan, examining the whimsical mushroom piece, didn't seem to notice, but Barrie knew the small proprietary gesture was made for her benefit. The flash of Tricia's blue eyes said Barrie might be the stained-glass expert, but *Tricia* had Jordan.

Mike had made the relationship between Jordan and Tricia sound strictly like an older guy chasing a younger girl. Barrie's impression was suddenly rather different. She saw a very clever girl out to ensnare an older man with her youth and innocence. Tricia was the chaser—discreetly, of course—as much as the chased.

The small byplay between Barrie and Tricia lasted only a moment. Then Barrie turned back to Vanessa. She told Barrie she had a client with a window which looked out on the blank wall of the next door apartment, and she thought a stained-glass window with cheerful colors would be just the solution. Vanessa said she would call Barrie later with the window measurements so Barrie could work out a price estimate on an enlarged version of the Mt. Hood scene.

Barrie left the luncheon meeting with mixed feelings. She was elated with Vanessa's enthusiastic approval of her work and the definite possibility of doing a window. Vanessa had also purchased the lake scene on the spot. But she was perplexed by the relationship between Jordan and Tricia. She hadn't caught passing between Jordan and Tricia any of the small but meaningful looks and gestures lovers usually exchange, but Tricia's hand on Jordan's arm was evidently a familiar enough gesture not to surprise him. However, he hadn't made any particular response to the touch . . .

Neither had he said a word about the date he had made with Barrie to drive up to Timberline Lodge on Saturday. He had evidently forgotten it or, considering the events of last weekend, decided to ignore it.

On Saturday morning, Barrie dressed in her usual working clothes, cut-off jeans and old cotton blouse. The owner of a specialty store she had visited after the luncheon had said he was interested in seeing samples of Christmas decorations done in stained glass, and she decided now to try something of that type.

One of her design books had a Santa Claus drawing, but it wasn't quite what Barrie wanted. She made some alterations in the design, and then, using graph paper, made a full-size drawing, called a cartoon. From the cartoon she cut a pattern, with each piece carefully numbered to correspond to the numbered pieces on the cartoon. The scissors were a special type that cut away a strip the exact width of the lead came that would be fitted around each piece of glass.

She made another copy of the cartoon and spread it flat on the table. She tacked it in place with two small boards at right angles around one corner. The cut pieces of glass would be fitted into place directly over this pattern, working outward from the corner where the boards were tacked.

Barrie was just preparing to start her first glass cut when a car pulled into the driveway. Jordan! She was so surprised, the carbide wheel glass cutters clattered to the floor. She nervously retrieved the tool and went to the door to answer Jordan's knock.

"I—I wasn't expecting you," she said lamely.

His blue eyes traveled appraisingly down to her bare legs, then back up again. Noting, she was sure, that she was braless beneath the loose blouse. "I can see that."

"At lunch you didn't mention anything about—"

"I told you last weekend I'd take you up to Timberline today. I don't say I'll do something and then not do it." His grim manner said he'd keep his word even if taking her up to the lodge were the last thing on earth he wanted to do. "Unless you've made other plans?"

Her first reaction was to tell him he needn't ruin his day on *her* account, but seeing a certain knowing look on his face, she changed her mind. She could keep her word just as stubbornly as he could.

"I said I'd go and I will." Barrie deliberately made her words a mocking echo of his. "I'll be ready in just a few minutes."

She hurriedly changed to burgundy-wine slacks and frilly

camisole blouse with a long-sleeved gauze overblouse.

"Better take a sweater," Jordan called. "It may be cool up there."

She added a quick touch of lipstick and mascara and was ready in little more than five minutes after Jordan's arrival. He looked surprised but made no comment.

The highway up the mountain, though winding and steep, was excellent. Their conversation was stiff and impersonal, limited to comments on the weather and spectacular mountain scenery. Jordan parked the car in the large parking area below the lodge. Clouds still obscured the top of the mountain, but the lodge and chair lift were in glorious sunshine.

"If you'd like to ride the chair lift, we should probably do that first," Jordan suggested as they walked across the parking lot. "The snow sometimes gets a little soft later in the day and there's not as much action on the ski slope then."

Barrie said that would be fine. Between the lower parking area and the main older lodge was a bulky concrete building which Jordan said would be used as a day lodge when it was completed. It would accomodate some of the services the older lodge now offered, restaurant and bar, warming area for skiers, and leave the older lodge for use mainly as a hotel.

The styles of the two buildings were in sharp contrast, Barrie realized as she got her first full view of the main Timberline lodge. The new day lodge was almost severely modernistic, the old lodge massively, magnificently baronial. It was built of stone and weathered wood, with a sharply sloped roof and massive chimney. The lower entrance was a cavelike archway in an imposing semicircle of stonework.

"We'll take a tour through the lodge later," Jordan said, guiding her lightly to the chair lift beyond.

Barrie had never ridden a chair lift before. Jordan purchased tickets, and the attendant motioned them inside the rope barrier. Barrie was surprised to find the chairs did not stop to let riders on. She had to step in place just after one chair glided by, and then the next one just swooped her up. She felt a little breathless as she clutched the orange metal center pole which anchored the double chair to the moving cable overhead.

"Okay?" Jordan asked lightly. He had stepped onto the opposite half of the chair with experienced ease.

"It's marvelous!" Barrie exclaimed, too delighted with the glorious feeling of gliding over the barren slope far below to remember to be cool and aloof.

Jordan offered a few statistics. Timberline Lodge was at a 6,000-foot elevation. The Magic Mile chair lift on which they were riding would take them to 7,000 feet. Beyond that the Palmer lift, for skiers only, went to 8,500-foot elevation. And beyond that the peak soared to over 11,000 feet. Mt. Hood was one of the most climbed peaks in the nation and had been safely climbed by young and old alike, and yet it wasn't very long ago that five climbers had met their deaths on its treacherous slopes. But today the mountain was a benevolent, slumbering giant, the peak now and then visible behind drifting fluffy clouds.

"It's so quiet," Barrie said dreamily. The silence was total except for the small hiss of the cable as the chair passed each of the huge black support poles marching up the mountain. Her feet dangled in space, giving her a wonderful, childlike feeling of freedom.

At the top of Magic Mile, attendants standing on either side helped them off the moving chair. From there, skiers transferred to the other lift to take them farther up the mountain. Jordan and Barrie walked down a sloping ramp and across the bare, rocky ground to where they could watch the skiers.

Here there were rivers of snow, long fingers of white reaching down the mountain on either side of the bare area where they stood. The skiers zig-zagged down from above, swooped around a gentle curve, and then glided gracefully up the ramp for another ride up the mountain.

"Do you ski?" Jordan asked.

"No, but I'd love to try!"

It was not, Barrie realized lamely as soon as her enthusiastic reply dropped into space, an offer. Merely a polite inquiry.

But even Jordan's cool reserve couldn't spoil her appreciation of the panorama of forested beauty spread out below or the rugged beauty of the mountain soaring above. The grandeur of nature emphasized her own mortal insignificance and pointed up the pettiness of their human quarrels and differences.

Did Jordan feel that? Barrie couldn't tell. His face was inscrutable as he gazed upward at the jagged crags and slopes, of snow scarred by trails of falling rock or ice.

They took a tour of the lodge after riding the chair lift down. The bottom level of the lodge was for skiers, a cave-like room centered with an enormous hexagonal fireplace. Everything about the lodge seemed to be built on some massive, larger-than-life scale. The newel posts by the stairs were sections of old telephone poles with the tops carved into animal shapes polished smooth by passing hands. The massive hexagonal fireplace continued upward through the main lobby, ninety-two feet from base to peak, and the huge supporting posts of the lofty ceiling were hexagonal also. There were photographs showing the lodge buried in snow so deep that skiers slid down the sloping roof. The main door, the lodge guide said, weighed eleven hundred pounds. It was a hand-hewn slab of ponderosa pine, five feet wide and ten feet high, supported by hand-forged hinges.

"I feel overwhelmed!" Barrie said finally when the tour was complete.

"But we didn't see the one thing you especially wanted to see, the Blue Ox bar." Jordan frowned. The guide had already disappeared. "Let's check at the information desk."

The college-age girl on duty at the information desk told them the Blue Ox was open for business only during the winter months. Guided tours usually went through the bar but today it was completely closed because of a leaky water pipe problem.

Jordan thanked the girl. As they walked out into the sunlight, he gave Barrie a sideways glance. "If you want to see the Blue Ox bar, it appears we'll have to come back this winter when it's open." After a meaningful pause, he added, "If you're still here this winter."

"I told you I'm staying at the cabin permanently," she retorted.

He raised a chestnut-bronze eyebrow. "Permanently?"

"Permanently."

The exchange of words was brief, but the sum total of what had been asked and answered added up to more than the brevity indicated. Jordan's frown changed to an almost self-conscious scowl.

"I suppose I *was* rather narrow-minded implying Mike was too young for you," he muttered.

"Perhaps you were," Barrie agreed. "Perhaps I . . . jumped to some uncalled for conclusions," she offered tentatively, without mentioning Tricia by name.

Jordan's mouth, straight and hard as chiseled stone when he was angry or remote, softened to an experimental smile. "Hungry?" he inquired.

"Starved!"

They went to the cafeteria on the bottom level of the lodge and selected hot chili and steaming coffee. They sat on opposite sides of a rectangular wooden table.

"I wonder if it's called Mount Hood because the top is so often hooded in clouds," Barrie mused as she removed her sweater. The icy reserve between them had thawed perceptibly, but it hadn't melted enough that Barrie felt safe with anything but neutral subjects.

"The mountain was named after a British naval officer," Jordan explained. "The Indians called it Wy'east and had a long myth surrounding it."

Barrie, crumbling crackers into her chili, looked up with interest.

"Wy'east and another mountain to the north known as Pa-toe were brothers, sons of the Great Spirit. A beautiful squaw mountain settled between them, and the brothers fought over her. The Great Spirit was a little annoyed with all the fireworks and banished her to a cave."

"That figures," Barrie murmured. "The woman always gets the blame."

Jordan raised an eyebrow but smiled and went on. "The Great Spirit set an ugly, toothless old woman named Loo-Wit, in the form of another mountain, to guard the stone bridge over the great river that separated the two brother mountains. But the squaw mountain, being perversely female, wouldn't stay put—"

Barrie quirked her mouth at the "perversely female" but didn't comment.

"—and she sneaked across the stone bridge to visit Wy'east. The brothers fought again and the natural bridge crashed. Pa-toe, today known as Mount Adams, won and the squaw mountain went back to slumber at his feet."

"With a good riddance from Wy'east?"

Jordan grinned. "Perhaps. But the real winner was Loo-wit. The Great Spirit decided to give her back her youth and beauty, and she became Mount Saint Helens, known far and wide for her breathtaking loveliness."

"And the recent postscript to the legend is that Mount Saint Helens has erupted, of course," Barrie mused as she sipped her coffee. "I wonder what that means?"

"Perhaps the moral to the story is—" Jordan paused and squinted thoughtfully into space "—Beware of beautiful young maidens because you never know when they're going to explode." There was a certain dancing gleam in his eyes as he added, "And you are a very beautiful young maiden."

"I take it you're drawing some conclusions?" she asked lightly.

"I've observed certain... ummm... explosive tendencies," he agreed. "I've resolved not to light matches at dangerous moments." When she didn't comment, he reached across the table and covered her hand with his. His blue eyes were suddenly intent and serious. "I'm not very good at making apologies, but that's what I'm trying to do. I'm not exactly proud of myself."

Barrie turned her hand over until her palm locked with his. "A mountain has nothing on you when you're angry." She was smiling but the words were tremulous. "I expected you to erupt fire and smoke any minute yourself."

He just grinned, and this time when they walked out of the lodge he was holding her hand in his. On the drive back down the mountain they parked at a trail marker and hiked back through the shadowed forest to a viewpoint. Along the trail, Jordan pointed out marks on some of the huge old stumps that showed the trees had been cut before the days of the modern chain saw, back when tree fallers balanced on springboards and attacked the giant trees with merely a crosscut saw and their own muscle.

"Back in the days when men were men?" Barrie suggested teasingly.

"I don't happen to have a crosscut saw along, but if it's proof of modern manhood you're looking for—"

With unexpected suddenness, Jordan paused in the middle of the pine-needle-padded trail. With an exaggerated leer, he swept her into his arms. His locked arms bent her backward from the waist in a grand, melodramatic gesture. His mouth ravished hers, lips grinding against hers, teeth clashing in a parody of pure macho dominance. Catching his spirit of playfulness, Barrie responded, running her fingers through his hair in wild abandon, heaving her chest in great gasping breaths. When his mouth released her, she threw her head back, surrendering her throat to his caresses.

"Take me!" she said. "Ravish me. I'm yours!"

Jordan chuckled and eased her to a straight standing position again. "Watch out," he whispered huskily, "or I might do it."

The kiss was just exaggerated play, but Barrie felt oddly breathless as she looked up into his laughing blue eyes. Her heart thudded as he leaned back against a tree, pulling her with him. She took a step forward to keep her balance, stepping between his braced legs into intimate contact with his body. There was nothing phony or melodramatically pretended about the flame that flickered inside her like the start of a wildfire.

"Are you enjoying yourself?" Jordan asked. He locked his hands behind her waist. "Not just pretending?"

Barrie was honestly bewildered. "Why would I pretend?"

"Keep a stiff upper lip? Make the best of a bad situation and all that?" He shrugged lightly.

Barrie shook her head helplessly. "Jordan, I—" Then she reached up with both hands and pulled his head down to hers. The kiss was deep and sweet, a hungry feasting that was both physically and emotionally satisfying. Barrie had the strange feeling that at this moment anything more would have been too much, a separating intrusion into a feeling that went beyond sexual desire. The kiss was enough in itself.

They were both silent on the walk back to the car. Jordan seemed lost in thought, but his hand never relaxed its grip on hers. A few uneasy thoughts drifted to the surface of Barrie's mind as they paused at a footbridge to watch a doe and spotted fawn grazing downstream. She and Jordan had each made tentative apologies for last weekend, and here in this idyllic setting it seemed as if nothing could possibly separate them.

And yet, was anything really settled? Resolutely, Barrie swept disquieting questions into a corner of her mind and closed a door on them. Today was too perfect to spoil with niggling worries. She would not *look* for dark shadows.

At the cabin, Barrie fixed shrimp salad and toast and resurrected the strawberry and ice cream dessert from the freezer where she had unhappily plopped it last weekend. Afterward they carried cups of coffee outside and sat on the porch steps in companionable silence. It was the time of day Barrie loved best . . . a few peaceful moments suspended in time as dusk deepened to darkness, when both world and personal problems seemed less pressing. A smoky wood scent lingered in the air, and a jumping fish sent a widening pattern of concentric circles rippling across the dark mirror surface of the lake.

"Let's walk along the lake and watch the moon come up." Jordan held out his hand and Barrie took it.

They strolled in peaceful silence. The moon, not yet risen, made an ethereal glow beyond the forested slopes. Selecting an unobstructed viewpoint, Jordan settled himself on the ground with his back against a tree. Barrie sat in front of him, inside the secure frame of his legs with her back against his chest and her head tucked under his chin. His hands slid under her blouse and rested with warm familiarity against the bare skin of her midriff.

"Barrie," he began hesitantly, "I want to get something straight before—"

Involuntarily Barrie stiffened. She didn't want to talk. At this moment she only wanted to feel the soothing warmth of his presence, to drift on this gentle tide of togetherness. The mountain shimmered, unreal and magical, backlighted by the moon beyond the horizon, so beautiful it made a strange little ache inside her. She lifted her hand and ran it lightly along the angular edge of his jaw.

Momentarily distracted, he turned his head and kissed her fingertips before continuing determinedly. "Before you get any more wrong ideas about Tricia. I suppose you could say we've dated. We've been together a lot this summer, but it's just a fun, uncomplicated relationship. Tricia is uncomplicated. She was raised on an isolated ranch in eastern Oregon, and she's more at home riding the range than chasing around the city. Everything is so new and marvelous to her. Taking her places is like showing a kid sister around. She has this refreshing, unjaded outlook on life and wants to sample everything."

Including handsome architects, Barrie thought wryly, but she didn't say anything. She wasn't convinced Tricia was quite as naive and dewy-eyed as Jordan thought, but she was willing to give the girl the benefit of the doubt. Jordan's attitude toward Tricia seemed benevolently protective, a bit fatherly... and there was nothing fatherly about the way his hands were roaming the curves of her own body. At some point he had unfastened the tiny pearl buttons of her blouse, and now exploring fingertips crept inside the cups of her bra and caressed the tips of her breasts to taut peaks. The already snug bra felt almost unbearably tight and restraining. She twisted to face him, and as she did so his hands unfastened the bra and her breasts spilled free against his chest. With the sudden freedom came another release, a gloriously reckless feeling that obliterated Tricia and all else. It snapped a cautious reserve that was holding her back. She placed her hands on his throat, feeling the surging throb of his pulse.

Her body was arched backward at a sharp angle that might have been painful under other circumstances, but she was hardly conscious of it now. Jordan slid down, easing his body, solid and warm, beneath hers. A faint ringing sound penetrated Barrie's consciousness... the phone, the damn phone, but it was far away and Jordan didn't seem to hear and eventually it stopped ringing . . . or perhaps the jarring sound was simply lost in the muffled thunder of her own heartbeat as Jordan's powerful arms lifted her bodily over him. With an exquisitely sensuous touch of his lips he caressed each rounded breast suspended above him, tantalizing her with the touch of his tongue until she felt as if her body were one yearning ache of longing. His legs wrapped around hers, imprisoning her against him, but she was already his willing captive.

Another sound vaguely penetrated the fog of her consciousness. "Jordan, stop!" she whispered frantically, trying to stop his movements with a thrust of her body. She lifted her head to focus on the sound. "Someone is coming along the trail!"

The rising moon had been forgotten, but now Barrie felt spotlighted by its silvery rays. And here she was, half-dressed, lying in Jordan's arms on the fragrant carpet of pine needles.

"Don't move," Jordan whispered. His strong grip lowered her body until her breasts rested intimately against his chest, and her contours fit into the hard angles and planes of his. He wrapped his arms around her, holding her so tightly she could scarcely breathe. She buried her face in his throat and closed her eyes, as if by so doing she was hidden from view. But she could hear the voices coming closer and closer . . . laughter . . . footsteps. Any moment she expected to hear a shocked gasp or snicker as they were spotted.

But somehow the fear of discovery, instead of taking away the desire that throbbed between them, only seemed to intensify it. Motionless, Barrie felt wild surging forces gathering within her, mounting toward some point of no return. She lowered her mouth to Jordan's, oblivious to all else, and when their lips finally parted there was only velvet silence around them.

"Wouldn't you have felt foolish if they had caught us?" she whispered tremulously. She felt laughter and relief all mixed up together.

He laughed too, that warm, husky chuckle that she loved. "I'm not sure I'd have known there was anyone within a mile if you hadn't told me." His mouth found an exquisitely sensitive point on her throat. "When I have you in my arms I can't think of anything else."

"Not even a nice, comfortable, private bed?" she asked in a teasing whisper.

"Is that an invitation?"

"If you don't know an invitation by now when you hear one—" Her voice held a mock severity, and he laughed again.

They returned to the cabin. It was dark except for silver shafts of moonlight angling through the windows. Taking Jordan's hand, Barrie led him around her worktable and into the bedroom. Beside the bed, he swung her back into his arms. The embrace was light, as if ready to release her.

"Are we rushing things?" he asked.

Barrie's voice was unsteady as she answered, "At the moment, rushing things is exactly what I have in mind."

Jordan picked her up and set her gently on the bed. And just at that moment the phone rang again. *Oh damn, damn, damn,* Barrie groaned inwardly. She had been so eager to have the thing installed and now she wished it would just quietly disintegrate.

Jordan was bent over the bed, his arms still cradling her. "Are you expecting a call?" His voice was suddenly flat and neutral.

"It's probably Vanessa. She was supposed to call with the window measurements we discussed at lunch."

Jordan groaned, but with resigned good humor he said, "You'd better answer it, then. If I know Vanessa, she'll just keep ringing until she gets you. We might appreciate the interruption even less a little later on," he added meaningfully.

Still Barrie hesitated, wishing the phone would just stop ringing and automatically solve the problem. It was a peculiar time for Vanessa to call. But she wasn't expecting any other calls, and surely the incredibly bad timing of last week couldn't repeat.

The phone rang on and on with monotonous regularity, as if it were prepared to ring steadily all night. If it were in the other room she might stubbornly ignore the ringing, but the phone was on a long cord and she had moved it into the bedroom last night. The shrill noise was only inches away. Reluctantly, Barrie finally fumbled for the receiver.

"Hello."

"Hello. Barrie? You sound a little peculiar. Are you all right?"

Barrie felt a spinning dizziness at the sound of Killian's voice. No, no, *no*. The one person she did not want to hear from. She pressed the phone against her ear with a painful pressure to prevent any sound of his voice from escaping.

"Yes, this is Barrie," she said, desperately stalling for time. She hated to deceive Jordan, but she *couldn't* let him know it was Killian on the other end of the line. Not again.

So far Jordan didn't seem to suspect. Against the silvery moonlight he was a charcoal silhouette, unbuttoning his shirt, shrugging it off powerful shoulders. The words Killian was saying held only a minute amount of her attention. She pressed the receiver ever more tightly against her ear, murmuring a noncommittal "ummm" or "oh" at appropriate intervals. Jordan was beside her now, deftly removing her already disheveled blouse until she was naked from the waist up.

Then, as if he had all the time in the world, he began a leisurely exploration of every inch of exposed skin with his lips. His hands were behind him, as if this were some special no-hands game. An inventively creative game that made her skin feel as if it had a million erotically sensitive nerve endings she'd never before known existed. Killian's voice kept fading away to meaningless noises as one tantalizing sensation after another crowded it out.

Once Killian stopped whatever it was he was saying and demanded to know if she had a cold. "Your breathing sounds uneven," he said in a reproving tone.

Uneven! Barrie felt as if she could hardly breathe at all. Her heart pounded wildly, and her eyes were so tightly squeezed shut that stars sparkled like fireworks behind her eyelids. Her breasts felt swollen and exquisitely sensitive. Jordan had added one hand to his game now, kneading and caressing the flat plane of her abdomen. Her body moved sinuously beneath his hand, arching and responding like a purring cat stroked to the point of bliss.

If Killian would just get to the *point*. Barrie groaned inwardly as he went on and on about some motel owner who had been to the house and admired the three-dimensional window she had done for the entryway. Who *cared?* She longed to slam the phone down and give herself up to the ecstasy of Jordan's caresses completely. But she was afraid Killian would angrily dial again, and Jordan would then realize who it was.

So far Jordan seemed to be too absorbed to pay much attention to her murmured end of the conversation. Then his mouth moved up to nibble her free ear and murmur wickedly, "Tell Vanessa you'll talk business some other time. Right now you have more important business with a very eager lover."

"Well, if that's everything . . ." Barrie murmured into the phone.

"What I'm trying to tell you," Killian said, sounding aggrieved, "is that Warrenton may be interested in commissioning you to do the stained-glass murals for the new bar and restaurant he's adding to the motel. He was very impressed with your three-dimensional work. Said it was very unusual. It sounds as if he wants a whole series of scenes, so it could be a very large and important job for you."

In spite of the wild distraction of Jordan's caresses, Barrie pushed herself to a half-sitting position on the bed, her attention suddenly riveted on Killian. "Are you sure?"

"He wants to meet you to discuss the project."

Barrie's mind raced. Murals of the magnitude Killian was talking about could easily run into the thousands of dollars and bring her important recognition. It was a fantastic, almost incredible opportunity. The long distance would be awkward, of course, but somehow she would manage.

"Where is the motel?" Barrie asked.

"It's near Atlantic City. Are you planning a trip back east any time in the near future?"

"No, but for something this important I could arrange a trip to Atlantic City, of course. When—"

Barrie broke off, suddenly aware that Jordan had straightened, and his sharply silhouetted figure showed fists clenched at his sides.

"Who the hell are you talking to?" There was an ominous, eye-of-the-hurricane quiet in his voice.

Barrie covered the mouthpiece. "It's Killian, but—"

He gave her no time to explain. "Somehow I didn't think it was Vanessa you were making plans to meet at a motel in Atlantic City." His voice dripped acid contempt. He snatched his shirt from the back of a chair and headed toward the door.

Barrie stared after him, momentarily too astonished to react. Killian's voice droned meaningless in her ear.

Barrie cut him off abruptly. "Killian, would you excuse me, please? Something has come up here. I'll have to talk to you later."

She slammed the phone down, astonishment at Jordan's reaction replaced by fury. She might have expected him to be annoyed by another call from Killian, but to jump to the conclusion that she would run back east to meet Killian at some Atlantic City motel was outrageous.

"Jordan!" she called.

The cabin shuddered under the savage slam of the outside door. Barrie scrambled off the bed, fumbling for her blouse, tripping over the long telephone cord. "Damn, damn..." she muttered in frustration as the cord tangled around her feet as if it were alive. How could he, how *dare* he, take a few overheard, out-of-context words and—"*Jordan!*"

She stumbled across the bedroom as an engine roared to life outside, banged her knee on the corner of the still unfamiliar storage bins along the living room wall. She raced to the door, yanked it open, and stood there helplessly as the roar of the engine echoed distantly through the stillness of the night.

chapter 7

BARRIE STARED AFTER the disappearing taillights, furious and frustrated. Damn him for his high-handed arrogance and unfair suspicions . . . damn Killian for calling at such a disastrous time . . .

She wasn't going to let Jordan get away with this. She stumbled into the bedroom and searched for her shoes and car keys. She was going to go over and tell him exactly what she thought of someone who jumped to conclusions without waiting for the facts.

She snapped the light on and blinked as the glare hurt her eyes. The bedspread was rumpled, the pillow crushed. The dial tone of the telephone hummed monotonously from where the receiver lay on the floor after her entanglement with the cord. Her unbuttoned blouse hung inside out over her naked breasts.

Somehow the light seemed to illuminate more than the disheveled scene. It shone into the corners of her mind and caught the image of Jordan in a glaring spotlight. Slowly she replaced the telephone, shutting off the mindless hum of the dial tone. Why should she run after Jordan with more explanations, more apologies? She had done nothing wrong, nothing for which she need apologize. And if her explanations hadn't gotten through to Jordan by now, they never would.

Stubbornly she waited by the window, watching for the lights in Jordan's house to flash on. When they didn't, some small part of her wondered hopefully if that meant he was returning to apologize. But he didn't return and the lights didn't go on, and she was left with the conclusion he had gone back to the Portland apartment. Back to fresh, unjaded Tricia?

In spite of her anger, Barrie toyed with the idea of calling Jordan at the apartment and explaining Killian's call. She even got as far as picking up the phone. But then the stubborn anger swept over her again. She shouldn't *have* to explain. Not again. A part of love was trust, a willingness to believe innocence until proven guilty.

But who ever said that what Jordan felt was *love*, she reminded herself bitterly. It was sex, raw and basic.

There was no sign of life around Jordan's place on Sunday morning. She called Killian back. He sounded a bit annoyed with her abrupt "emergency" of the night before, but he gave a spare-me-the-details sigh when she murmured something vague about problems with the cabin. He didn't know much more about the restaurant murals than he had told her on the phone last night. Warrenton was out of the country on business just now, but Killian would talk to him again when he returned, now that he knew Barrie was definitely interested. When Barrie suggested Killian just tell her how she could contact Warrenton herself, he offered some evasive excuses. Then in a more intimate tone, he went on to say that her trip back east would give the two of them an opportunity to get together and talk, that perhaps they had been too hasty in resorting to divorce to solve their problems.

Finally Barrie got the picture. She should have known he wasn't doing this merely as some generously helpful gesture. For whatever reasons, he was having thoughts about a reconciliation and was dangling the plum of an introduction to Warrenton in front of her with the idea of getting something in return.

No way, she thought resolutely. She had no desire at all to see Killian, much less return to the dead marriage.

But neither did she intend to let this tremendous oppor-

tunity elude her. Doing the restaurant murals was truly a
dream job, something she could hardly have hoped for until
she was much better established in her craft. On the trip
east, she would convey her appreciation in words to Killian
for his help but make it plain that was as far as her gratitude
went.

Crisply she suggested that when Warrenton returned to
the country, Killian set up a definite date when she could
meet him to discuss the project.

Vanessa called Monday morning with her client's window measurements. Barrie worked out a price and called
Vanessa back. Vanessa thought her client would find the
price acceptable and then called once more with a firm go-
ahead for Barrie to start work on the window. Before hanging up this time, Vanessa said her granddaughter was vis-
iting from back east and she was planning a picnic for the
girl's birthday on Saturday. Would Barrie like to come
along? They were going to a picnic area on a creek out near
the mountain.

"Why, how nice of you to invite me." Barrie was surprised and pleased with Vanessa's friendly invitation. "I'd
love to go. May I bring something?"

"No, I don't think so. I'm taking care of the food and
Tricia is arranging for horses. My granddaughter is just
crazy over horses, and I'm afraid her visit here has been
something of a disappointment so far." Vanessa laughed
ruefully. "Portland isn't exactly the Wild West that Karen
was hoping for. So I promised her this ride for her birthday."

Somehow the thought that Tricia would undoubtedly be
along on the picnic had escaped Barrie in her first flush of
pleasure at the unexpected invitation. And *horses?* "I'm
afraid I've never ridden anything larger or more challenging
than a pony at a carnival," she said, tactfully trying to
disentangle herself from the hasty commitment. "And I
haven't any riding clothes. So perhaps I shouldn't—"

"Nonsense." Vanessa cheerfully brushed those problems
aside. Tricia could arrange a nice, gentle horse for her, and
the only riding clothes she'd need were jeans and a comfortable shirt. Tricia could loan her a pair of western riding
boots. Vanessa added that they would be bringing the horses

in trailers and would meet her at the lake store on Saturday morning.

"Well, I'll see you then," Barrie finally agreed lamely. Hesitantly, trying to sound casual, she added, "Will I know any of the other guests?"

"Probably not. They're mostly some horsey-type friends of Tricia's. Oh, and Jordan Steele of course."

Of course, Barrie echoed silently.

Barrie resolutely tried to put her apprehensions about the coming weekend out of her mind and concentrate on construction of the window. It was larger than anything she had done recently, and she had to plan bracing rods to give the window structural strength without interfering with the artistic design.

Sometimes she thought the project was completely jinxed. At other times she unhappily suspected that although she might be keeping her conscious mind off the coming weekend, her subconscious was sending frantic distress signals through her fumbling fingers. She should never have accepted the invitation without checking details first. She should have found some way to back out gracefully. Why hadn't Tricia stopped her aunt from inviting Barrie? The obvious answer was that Vanessa had issued the invitation without consulting Tricia. How would Jordan react to her presence?

On Saturday Barrie dressed in jeans, plaid blouse, and sneakers. She drove to the store early, taking along a small gift she had made for Vanessa's granddaughter. Vanessa arrived with the van a few miniutes later. It was loaded with food and ice chests and folding chairs. Vanessa gaily said that this was her maiden voyage, her first time driving since her broken leg. Tricia and Vanessa's granddaughter and the others had gone on ahead with the horses. No mention of Jordan.

But Jordan, of course, was the first person Barrie spotted as the van pulled into the picnic area near a creek. He stood out even in the colorful, noisy jumble of horses and people. Or was it just that she couldn't see anyone else when he was around?

He was just swinging onto the back of a sleek black horse. He looked ruggedly masculine astride the nervous horse, soothing it with a firm but gentle hand on the reins and a calming pat on its muscular neck. Another rider on a gray horse dashed up, horse's white mane and girl's golden hair both flying loose and carefree. The spirited horse tossed its head impatiently, and the girl flung her hair out of her eyes with an equally spirited gesture. Horse and rider made a perfect picture of overflowing youthful energy and vitality and beauty. Barrie's knowledge of horses was minuscule, but she recognized the classic Arabian head on Tricia's mount. Recognized, too, the lithe expertise with which Tricia spun the horse in a half circle and raced up to the van.

Barrie watched the horse dance sideways and toss its head, nostrils flaring. Was she going to be expected to ride something like *that?* There was a reckless sparkle in Tricia's blue eyes that made Barrie distinctly uneasy. Would Tricia deliberately give her a mount that was beyond her ability to handle?

"Your horse is tied on the other side of that blue horse trailer," Tricia said to Barrie. "And there's an extra pair of boots in the pickup."

Barrie glanced uneasily around the scene. The setting was gorgeous: sparkling creek, stately evergreens, the magnificent backdrop of the looming mountain. The air smelled of dust and pine and horseflesh. Horses whinnied and a pickup door banged, and hooves thudded from inside a horse trailer. There were more people than Barrie had expected, and each one seemed to know exactly what to do and how to do it.

"Perhaps I should just stay here and help with the food," Barrie demurred.

"Nonsense. You run along and have fun," Vanessa said gaily. "The old folks like me are going to sit around and play poker. I see Karen is already riding like a wild Indian." A little sandy-haired girl of about eleven or twelve flew by on the back of a stocky bay horse.

Reluctantly Barrie followed Tricia to the pickup, noting out of the corner of her eye that Jordan had dismounted and was doing something with the cinch on his saddle. He didn't look in her direction.

The loaned boots didn't fit. They were too small, making Barrie immediately feel large and ungainly next to Tricia. Her mount also looked enormous, standing several inches taller than Tricia's trim gray. The feeling of ungainly awkwardness did not improve as Barrie clambered onto the back of the big brown horse. He stood patiently, however, never moving as she struggled into the saddle.

"His name is Duke and all the kids ride him." Tricia flashed a brilliant smile. "So you shouldn't have any problems." Then, hair flying like some desert princess, she galloped off to join Vanessa's granddaughter.

Barrie nudged the big horse with the heels of her sneakers. He ambled off, reaching down to snatch a mouthful of grass as they passed a tall clump. Barrie was relieved to find that he neither pranced nor danced, and he stolidly ignored other horses loping by. Barrie tentatively applied the reins and murmured a hopeful "Whoa," and the creature agreeably stopped. Barrie let out a long, tense breath. She might manage to survive this day yet, though her knees already felt uncomfortable.

But perhaps her suspicions of Tricia had been unwarranted, she thought guiltily. Duke *was* calm and gentle.

"You shouldn't ride in shoes like that. Your foot might slip through the stirrup and get caught."

Barrie twisted in the saddle at the sound of the disapproving voice. Her eyes met Jordan's beneath the curved brim of his straw cowboy hat. A jaunty feather decorating the hat gave him a rakish look that was not matched by his unsmiling face.

"Are your stirrups the right length?" Jordan asked.

"I don't know." Barrie hesitated then finally admitted, "I don't know how long they're supposed to be."

"Stand up in them."

Barrie obeyed, balancing herself with one hand on the horn while her derriere wobbled above the saddle. Jordan dismounted and looped the black horse's rein's around a tree. He efficiently lifted the stirrup leather and adjusted something underneath to change the length, then repeated the maneuver on the other side. Barrie was acutely conscious of his hands brushing her legs as he worked, but the contact had no effect on his coolly impersonal air.

"Try that."

With the stirrups lengthened, Barrie's knees were no longer uncomfortably bent. "Thank you. That's much better."

"I take it you haven't ridden much?" His eyes appraised her uncertain grip on the reins and carefully held balance.

Barrie was very much aware of Tricia and Vanessa's granddaughter racing in reckless circles around the flat next to the creek. Duke stood with his head down, eyes half-closed.

"No I haven't." With a glance toward the flying figures, she added defiantly, "But I'll manage."

Jordan untied his horse and swung into the saddle again. "I'm surprised to see you here today."

"I'm sorry if my presence makes you uncomfortable," Barrie said stiffly. "Evidently Vanessa doesn't know the . . . complete situation or she wouldn't have invited me."

"I wasn't referring to that. I assumed you had other plans for this weekend." He flashed her a derisive smile. "Such as a rendezvous at a motel in Atlantic City."

"Obviously your assumptions are not always correct," Barrie snapped.

He scowled but made no reply and abruptly spurred the horse into a lope away from her. Barrie bit her lip as she watched him join the zestful group playing tag on horseback. If he had bothered to ask, she would have told him about the business nature of Killian's call. But she would not beg him to listen to an explanation.

When everyone was saddled and ready, Tricia took over as a kind of trail boss and organized the ride. Barrie started out near the middle of the line of riders, but first one rider and than another passed her on the trail. Embarrassed, Barrie tried to urge the horse to go faster, but he had one speed. Slow. Duke obviously hadn't a competitive bone in his body and was quite content to straggle along at the end of the line, snatching a bite of grass whenever he could. Once, at a particularly succulent clump, he stopped completely and no amount of kicking or frantic clucking by Barrie would induce him to move. Jordan rode back to see what was wrong.

"Don't let him do that," Jordan said sharply as the horse continued to chomp on the grass. "Yank his head up when he tries to eat."

"I am yanking." Barrie blinked back tears of frustration. "He doesn't pay any attention."

Jordan reached down and gave the reins a sharp jerk. Duke looked mildly surprised and for a few minutes paid attention to business. Jordan loped back toward the head of the line.

Duke reverted to his former ways. Barrie's bare ankles were sore from rubbing on the stirrups, and her legs ached from constantly urging the horse to keep up with the others. The magnificent setting, golden shafts of sunlight streaming through the trees and the cool, damp scent of shadowy glades, was lost on her. She discovered Duke's placid, unexcitable nature also covered an obstinate determination to go exactly where *he* wanted, which included a shortcut under some low branches that tangled in Barrie's hair and scratched her arms.

Finally Barrie decided she'd had enough. She would turn around and go back to the picnic area. She had the unpleasant feeling everyone was watching and snickering at her incompetence. She hauled the horse around in a wide circle, nothing like the spinning turns Tricia made on her little Arabian. Duke ambled along for several hundred yards before a whinny from the group evidently brought him to the startled realization that he was *alone*. With unexpected agility he whirled and started at a rough trot back toward the now out of sight group of riders. It was all Barrie could do to hang on, teeth jarring mercilessly with each bounce of the horse's rough gait. Her hair was disheveled and her ankles raw by the time Duke got close enough to the others to satisfy him. Then he slowed to his usual plodding walk.

The horses were crossing a low-lying, grassy meadow

now, and Barrie actually caught up with the other riders when they stopped to let their horses take a few sips of water where the trail crossed a meandering stream. Duke plodded right into the water and lowered his head to drink.

"Don't let him drink too much," Jordan warned, suddenly appearing at her side like some disapproving guard. "Too much water can make a hot horse sick."

Barrie pulled on the reins, but her arms were already exhausted from trying to slow that bone-jarring trot. But Duke evidently wasn't very thirsty, and after a moment he started sloshing his mouth in the stream, throwing water from side to side. Then he pawed with one foot, raising the hoof high and flailing the water into a muddy froth with an almost devilish glee. What in the world was *wrong* with him, Barrie wondered frantically. He felt strangely wobbly.

"Watch out!" Jordan warned. "He's going to—"

Before Jordan could finish the warning, the horse did what he intended to do. His front end dipped down, then his hind, and then he flopped down on his side. Barrie, already loose in the saddle, tumbled sideways into the water. The stream wasn't more than a foot and a half deep, but she went under and came up gasping and sputtering. She sat there in the muddy water watching in astonishment through wet hair plastered to her face as the horse squirmed and rolled in the water with apparent relish.

Jordan splashed his horse toward her. "Are you all right?"

Barrie wiped the wet hair out of her eyes. Her muddy hands left equally muddy streaks on her face. With as much dignity as she could muster, she stood up. "I'm fine." Her wet clothes were plastered to her body and her feet lost in a muddy ooze. The horse stood up, spraying her again as he shook himself. The saddle was covered with mud.

Tricia loped back from the head of the line of riders that had already started into the trees on the far side of the meadow. "What happened?" she gasped. "I had no idea you wouldn't be able to handle Duke. The children love him!"

Tricia's face was registering surprise and concern, but Barrie was certain there was a gleam of high glee in her eyes that matched Duke's glee in the water. Barrie's own expression was murderous as she snatched at the reins trailing in the water and led the horse up the slippery bank of the creek.

"I'm going back to the picnic area," Barrie announced flatly.

"We're over halfway," Jordan said. "It will be just as fast to finish out the ride."

"It's too bad we haven't any dry clothes along, or anything to wipe off the saddle." To Barrie's ears, Tricia's sweetly spoken regret was as phony as saccharin.

Barrie grimly scraped as much mud off the saddle as she could with her bare hands. Out of the corner of her eye she saw Jordan start to dismount, evidently to help her get back on the horse, and anger propelled her to jam her left foot into the stirrup and swing her right leg over the horse's back with more confidence than she really felt.

She sat rigidly straight in the saddle as they caught up with the others, gritting her teeth and ignoring the uncomfortable rubbing of skin against wet clothes and muddy saddle. Her feet felt squishy in the wet sneakers. Tricia loped up to the head of the line again. Jordan remained behind Barrie, evidently to prevent further disasters. She ignored him.

After a short but steep climb over a rocky ridge, the line paused to let the horses catch their breath. An older man sympathetically eyed Barrie's wet, muddy condition and smiled.

"Old Roller did it again, did he? That's one of his favorite tricks with an inexperienced rider. But he's a pretty good horse if you just let him know who's boss."

"I'm afraid he *knows* who's boss," Barrie said unhappily. And so did Tricia, she thought with an explosion of anger. Tricia knew exactly what kind of horse she was getting for Barrie. She had deliberately calculated to ridicule and humiliate Barrie, and her plans couldn't have worked out better. Barrie had unwittingly supplied the comic relief for the ride.

Duke either anticipated the end of the ride or sensed Barrie's angry determination, because his ears perked up and he kept up with the other horses. They had to recross the creek to return to the picnic area. This time Barrie broke a switch off a willow bush, and when the horse paused in the center of the stream, evidently considering another refreshing roll, she snapped him smartly across the rump. He gave a grunt of surprise and splashed on through the water. The small victory gave Barrie a certain sense of satisfaction, but it didn't help her raw spots or aching muscles.

She silently turned Duke over to Tricia and squished her way to the van. Inside, she stripped off her clothes and Vanessa rinsed them in the creek and spread them on a bush to dry in the sun. Vanessa also rounded up a man's denim jacket for Barrie to put on, plus a blanket to cover her from the waist down. Decently if not fashionably covered, Barrie ate her picnic dinner of fried chicken and cole slaw perched on a rock beside the van. Afterward there was a candle-covered chocolate cake for the birthday girl and the opening of some presents. Vanessa's granddaughter was surprised and delighted with Barrie's handmade gift, a mobile of little dancing horses made from scraps of stained glass.

After a brief rest, the indefatigable horsey people were ready to ride again. This time they stayed on the flat near the creek, playing games on horseback. Races carrying a boiled egg on a spoon, musical chairs in which the riders flung themselves off their horses with what seemed to Barrie incredibly wild abandon, races weaving through a makeshift line of poles. Barrie sat watching from the van, and Vanessa joined her. They carried on a casual conversation about the games, with Vanessa adding a sprinkling of information about this or that guest. The middle-aged Butlers owned the Arabian mare Tricia was riding. In her spare time Tricia had been training a couple of young horses for them this summer.

"I wonder where she found Duke for me," Barrie murmured.

Vanessa laughed. "I don't know, but I'm sure she feels terrible about the choice."

Barrie doubted that, but didn't comment. Jordan and Tricia were now working as a team in something Vanessa called a rescue race, in which one rider swung on behind the other.

"It's good to see Jordan laughing and having such a good time," Vanessa murmured. Her mouth curved in a maternalistic smile.

"Doesn't he usually enjoy himself?" Barrie asked, surprised. Jordan's husky chuckle was one of the special things she had loved about him.

"He didn't seem able to have much fun when I first met him two—no, I guess it's been almost three years now. He was really despondent."

"I think he was unhappy with the work he was doing in California."

"That too, I suppose, but it was something more personal. Something about a girl who gave him a really raw deal." Vanessa shook her head ruefully. "Jordan is one of the most attractive men I know, but he certainly hasn't been lucky in love. First his marriage, and then this other girl pulling such a similar trick on him. But I'm sure you know all about that. He said he's known you a long time. Tricia has been good for him, don't you think?"

Barrie managed to make some sort of noncommittal noise, but her mind was racing back and forth over Vanessa's casual comments. Comments that aroused more questions than they answered.

"Did you know his wife in California?" Vanessa added idly. "Oh-oh, there goes my granddaughter."

The little girl went flying off her horse on a sharp turn, but with youthful resilience she bounced back up before anyone could help her. A moment later she was back on the horse and racing around at breakneck speed again.

"No, I never met Jordan's wife," Barrie murmured. Jordan had evidently made some vague comments to Vanessa about knowing Barrie in the past, and Vanessa had assumed that meant they had known each other in California before he moved to Oregon. Vanessa also assumed, Barrie realized uneasily as the older woman went on, that Barrie knew considerably more about Jordan's personal life than she actually did.

"That wife must have been a real bitch to do what she did," Vanessa declared, using the word with spirited conviction. "Marrying Jordan just to spite some other guy when she was angry with him. Sneaking around behind Jordan's back to chase around and then divorce Jordan so she could marry the other guy."

Barrie was stunned. She had known Jordan had been married and divorced, of course, but he'd never confided any of the details. "Do you think he still cares for her?" Barrie asked tentatively.

"Oh, no. He got over her a long time ago. It was the *next* one who really did him in. That happened just before I met him, I think."

Two or three years ago, Barrie thought with a peculiar sinking sensation in her stomach. "Did he tell you what happened?"

"Oh, he met this girl and fell for her like the proverbial ton of bricks." Vanessa spoke almost absentmindedly, her eyes fondly following her granddaughter. "She strung him along for a while. I don't know all the details, of course— you know how closemouthed Jordan is—but I gather that she led him to believe she was divorced. But she wasn't and she blithely went back to her husband, quite unscathed I'm sure, and Jordan was practically wiped out. He was really in love with her."

"There could have been . . . extenuating circumstances." Barrie's voice came out so strained that Vanessa gave her a sharp glance. Barrie ran a nervous hand over her tight throat. "Perhaps I—I'm catching a cold."

"Would you like a cup of hot coffee? Or a glass of lemonade?"

Barrie shook her head. "No. Thanks anyway. I'll load up on vitamin C when I get home." She glanced at Vanessa out of the corner of her eye and tried to keep her voice as casual as the older woman's. "Do you think he's over this other girl now too?"

"Oh, I suppose so. After all, it's been at least three years. But with a guy like Jordan, it's hard to know . . ." Vanessa frowned slightly as her voice trailed off.

Barrie was flooded with waves of mixed emotions as she watched without really seeing the exuberant action of the horseback games. One part of her felt a lilting joy. She knew for certain now that Jordan really had been in love with her once. It hadn't been just fantasy or wishful thinking on her part. And in spite of the conflicts and doubts between them, she also felt certain something of that emotion remained in Jordan. That any feeling could remain after all that had happened was a tribute to the depths of what Jordan was capable of feeling.

His first wife had deserted him to go back to her former love. And then Barrie had done almost exactly the same thing. At least from Jordan's viewpoint that was what she had done. No wonder he had darkly brooding suspicions!

Barrie felt a sharp sense of elation and excitement as she saw everything from a new perspective. A man would have to be stupid or insensitive not to react with wariness and suspicion under the circumstances, and Jordan was neither. Infuriatingly stubborn sometimes, she thought with a breathless little smile, but intelligent and sensitive, and sweet and loving . . .

Barrie was so lost in her own inner excitement that she had to clasp her hands together under the blanket to keep them from trembling. She caught only the tail end of something Vanessa was saying.

". . . young for him, but she's maturing rapidly." Vanessa smiled fondly and sighed. "Oh, to be nineteen and in love again."

"You think Tricia is in love with Jordan?" Barrie ventured.

"What do you think?" Vanessa nodded toward the creek where Tricia was gaily splashing Jordan with water. Barrie felt a sharp pang as he grabbed the laughing girl and playfully ducked her face under the water.

"I wonder how he feels about her."

"Oh, so far I think he just looks on her as kind of a cute kid. But one of these days he'll wake up and notice her. A man like Jordan, strong and self-reliant as he is, isn't the kind to live without love. But I think he'll be very careful not to get burned again." Vanessa's voice was thoughtful, and then she laughed lightly. "At least he won't have to worry about Tricia running back to an old husband or boyfriend. Her only past loves have been horses."

"But she still has three years of college to finish, doesn't she?" Barrie asked. "And the fall term will be starting soon."

"I'm not sure Tricia will go back to college this fall," Vanessa said thoughtfully. "She wasn't really very happy there. And if she does, Oregon State isn't all that far away, of course."

"Of course," Barrie echoed. She swallowed uneasily. "You don't think Jordan is too old for her?"

"My husband was seventeen years my senior. He's been dead six years now, so I suppose there are some drawbacks when you consider the years alone." Vanessa's voice was husky as she added softly, "But the years when he was alive were worth it."

So the relationship between Jordan and Tricia had Vanessa's blessing, Barrie realized. She was biting her lip, feeling all jumbled up inside, when Vanessa glanced over at her.

"They would both be furious if they knew we were talking about them like this."

"I certainly won't mention it," Barrie managed to mutter faintly.

Vanessa went to retrieve Barrie's clothes from the bush as the group began unsaddling and loading horses into trailers in preparation to end the day. Barrie sat waiting, uneasily mulling over Vanessa's words. This explained so much that had puzzled her about Jordan's suspicions, but the last few moments talking with Vanessa had also given her yet another perspective on the situation, one in which she was less than comfortable. Unhappily, she saw herself as some wicked divorcee getting in the way of pure young love.

She suddenly remembered that first night Jordan had come to her cabin, and his somber statement about no one ever being really free of the past. She couldn't erase her past, and he couldn't change his. . . . Would it be better for Jordan, she wondered in dismay, if she just faded quietly out of the picture?

But she could not let him go on believing she was considering a rendezvous or reconciliation or *anything* with Killian. Even if Jordan never wanted her, he mustn't go on believing she was like his former wife, untrustworthy and underhanded, or that all women who had loved once were forever tied to the past.

And the first step was to swallow her stubborn pride and tell Jordan what that phone call from Killian was really all about.

chapter 8

NOW THAT BARRIE had made up her mind to explain to
Jordan about Killian's telephone call, she was eager to *do*
it. Jordan's house remained frustratingly dark that evening.
Evidently he was spending the night in the Portland apartment again. Alone? Yes. She was reasonably certain by
now that his relationship with Tricia was not a physically
intimate one. That thought should have reassured her, but
somehow it did not, and she spent a restless night tossing
and turning.

Sunday morning was surprisingly chilly, with a definite
end-of-summer feeling in the crisp morning air. She would
have to see about buying a supply of wood for the fireplace
soon.

She spent the morning cleaning, but paused every now
and then to peer out the window and check Jordan's house
for signs of life. By midafternoon she had pretty well given
up hope and decided to take a swim. The afternoon was
sultry hot, in sharp contrast to the morning chill, and clouds
hung ominously around the mountain.

She enjoyed the swim, of course, enjoyed the feel of
cool water slipping like liquid silk over her skin, enjoyed
the exhilarating feeling of competence and confidence in
her body that a swim always gave her. But today something
was lacking. There was an emptiness, a loneliness. She
wasn't totally alone. Some hikers on the lake trail stopped

for a friendly chat. Boaters waved. But she felt . . . alone.

She was toweling herself dry when she glanced across the lake one more time. Her heart turned a little flip-flop. Jordan's car was in the driveway, a silvery gleam under the now overcast sky. Quickly she went inside and dressed. She had planned to hike around the lake to talk to him, making the stop at his place appear casually unplanned, but suddenly she was too impatient and took the car instead. Her stubbornness in not explaining that phone call with its incriminating mention of a motel meeting in Atlantic City now seemed childishly petulant.

Barrie braked in dismay halfway down the driveway to Jordan's house. He was not alone. A pickup that she hadn't been able to see from across the lake was backed into the garage. Jordan and another man were unloading some small pieces of furniture. And Tricia, lithe and long-legged in brilliant red short shorts, was laughingly supervising.

Barrie's first impulse was to jerk the gearshift into reverse and back out of the driveway before anyone saw her, but it was already too late for that. All three had stopped work and were looking curiously at her motionless car. Reluctantly she drove on down the driveway. Jordan wiped his hands on his jeans and came out to meet her.

"I didn't know you had company," Barrie faltered.

"Just some friends helping move some small things out from the apartment. The moving van will bring the large furniture later on."

"Oh." Barrie's hands clutching the steering wheel felt sweaty. "I just wanted to talk to you for a few minutes. I'll try to catch you sometime when you're not so busy."

Jordan glanced back at Tricia and the other man. Tricia was leaning against the pickup, her face innocently wide-eyed but her stance definitely provocative. Jordan shrugged lightly. "It's time for a break. We can talk in my office." His eyes held a warily curious expression.

"No. Some—some other time perhaps."

Before Jordan could say anything more, she wheeled the car in a tight circle and headed out the driveway. She had a quick mental image of Jordan and his friends having a hearty laugh over her peculiar behavior.

She drove around aimlessly for a while, wandering through a hillside of homes tucked away among the trees with only an elaborate gate or flash of glass wall hinting at the expensive elegance within. The air had a muggy before-a-storm feeling. The mountain had disappeared in the overcast sky, and the lake gleamed like dull metal.

Finally she went back to the cabin and worked on the window again, resolutely not even glancing across the lake. She fixed a cold sandwich for supper, first washing her hands thoroughly to be certain no trace of lead came remained. Afterward, to the rumble of thunder, she went back to work, ready to start soldering the joints on the window design.

Just before dark she heard a car pull up in front of the cabin and stop. At the same time, a jarring flash of lightning shook the house. As if it were some cosmic signal, an abrupt downpour started. She knew instinctively, without going to the window, that the car was Jordan's. Her hands were suddenly trembly and she had to set the soldering iron back on its holder to keep from making an unsightly blob of the joint.

She waited tensely for his knock, then called to him to come in. He stepped inside, bringing with him an aura of outdoor vigor and the scent of fresh rain. His hair glistened with droplets, and his cream-colored knit shirt was spattered with damp spots. He slanted a chestnut eyebrow quizzically.

"You wanted to talk to me?"

Her rehearsed speech felt foolish now. Did he even care? Perhaps he had been relieved by the excuse to stalk out. "I thought you'd probably gone back to Portland by now." An inane comment, since he was obviously here.

"No." He hesitated slightly. "Tricia and Guy didn't leave until just a few minutes ago."

Barrie walked back to the worktable and picked up the brush with which to apply flux to a joint before soldering. Outside the downpour continued, the staccato drum of rain on the old roof underscored by intermittent rumbles of thunder. She was jittery and had to keep her hands busy while she went through her explanation. "What I wanted to talk to you about—"

Jordan walked around the table so he could see the mountain scene in its proper upright position. "That's very good," he commented. "It's quite recognizable as Mount Hood, not just any mountain." He touched the jagged outcropping of Illumination Rock. "Where do you get your designs?"

Barrie gave him a sharp, surprised glance. He was obviously detouring her talk. "I did this one myself, working from a photograph of the mountain." She showed him the original cartoon, with each pattern piece carefully marked with a number and color.

"More work goes into a design of stained glass than most people realize," he commented. "What are you doing now?"

"I'm just starting the soldering. Each joint, where one strip of lead came meets another strip, must be soldered together."

"This is the material you refer to as lead came?" He picked up a long strip of the metal and experimentally molded it into an awkward curve. "Not so easy to do," he commented.

Barrie explained that each piece of lead came had to be stretched slightly before use. She put one end of the strip in a small vise, gave it a smooth, even pull with a pair of pliers, cut off a short length with her special leading knife, and deftly fit the strip along the edge of a scrap of stained glass. The lead came had a channel along each side into which the glass fit.

"That's an odd word: *came*," Jordan mused.

"It's an old English word meaning string or length," Barrie explained. "So lead came is a length of lead."

"Is the solder also lead?"

"I use what is called sixty-forty. Sixty percent lead, forty percent tin."

The conversation was so impersonal. Jordan's questions showed a genuine enough interest, but Barrie had the feeling they were using discussion of her work to skirt the real issue, tiptoing the edges as if it were some yawning chasm which might swallow them both.

"Do you have to do anything special for a large piece like this?" he inquired.

"I'll have to add bracing rods to give the window structural strength, something I don't have to do with smaller pieces, of course."

"It takes a perfectionist," Jordan observed. "I doubt that I'd have the patience."

"I don't think you could list patience as one of your virtues," Barrie agreed wryly.

Jordan scowled. He moved around to the far side of the table, deliberately putting distance between them. The thunder had faded away, but a sudden tension charged the air, as if an electrical current had passed through the room and polarized them into opposing camps. The fine hair on Barrie's arm prickled as she reached for the soldering iron. She kept her eyes on her work, but she was aware of Jordan folding his arms in a hostile stance.

"I came to see you today because I wanted to explain to you about Killian's call." Carefully keeping her voice nonaccusing, she added, "You ran out of here before I had a chance to explain."

"I'd say the call was self-explanatory."

"It wasn't!" Barrie said hotly, her resolve to stay calm forgotten. "You jumped to conclusions—*again*." She set the soldering iron back on the holder. "Killian called because a friend of his, a man named Warrenton, saw some of my stained-glass work and may be interested in commissioning me to do some large murals for him. Mr. Warrenton owns a motel near Atlantic City and is planning to add a restaurant and bar. He would like me to come back east and discuss the project with him. I know my end of the phone conversation with Killian sounded incriminating, but you had no right to think what you did!"

Jordan's reaction to her explanation was impossible to read. He was still scowling slightly, looking at her with narrowed eyes. A sudden clap of returning thunder made her jerk nervously, but he didn't so much as twitch a muscle. Wind-blown rain beat against the window, and his reflection in the dark glass looked menacingly formidable.

"And that's absolutely all Killian said?" Jordan asked

skeptically. "Nothing personal? Somehow I hadn't thought of him as being so solicitous about your work."

Barrie hovered on the edge of lying to him, or at least evading a direct answer. But she didn't want there to be any lies between them, not even on as quicksand a subject as this one. "Killian suggested we should get together and talk while I'm back there," she said reluctantly.

"And you agreed?"

"No! Of course not—"

"Then you refused?"

Barrie stared at the twist of a mocking smile on his face, angrily aware she had been backed into a corner. "Not exactly. I mean, I don't intend to talk to him about—" Barrie broke off. She didn't like even to refer to Killian and herself as an *us*. She swallowed and took a steadying breath. "About the divorce, but I will probably have to see him in order to get the introduction to Mr. Warrenton."

"I see."

"It's a fantastic opportunity—"

"Of course." The taunting smile and lift of eyebrows questioned to which opportunity she was referring: the chance to meet Warrenton or the chance to see Killian again.

"You're being totally unfair!" Barrie exploded. "You're suspicious of *me* just because—"

She stopped herself abruptly. If Jordan had wanted her to know the painful details of his marriage, he would have told her. Since he hadn't told her, she had no right to bring it up. It was unfair of him to be suspicious of her because of what some other woman had done to him in the past, unfair to suspect there was a possibility she would go back to Killian again because she'd been forced to do it once. Unfair—and yet painfully understandable. Eyes half-blinded with tears as she struggled for control, she reached for the soldering iron.

A blazing pain shot through her hand. She jerked it back and stared at the seared mark on her palm. In her agitation, she had grabbed not the handle but the hot tip of the soldering iron. She gripped her wrist with her other hand, as if that could somehow shut off the burning pain.

"Let me see!" Jordan commanded. He spread her curled fingers lightly. Barrie bit her lip and blinked back tears. "Better run cold water on it immediately."

They went into the kitchen, Barrie still holding her wrist as if the seared hand were some foreign object she was carrying. Jordan turned on the faucet. She put her hand under the cold stream, but she was trembling. Jordan reached around her and steadied her hand with his firm grip. He stood behind her, his body pressed against her back as the chill water from the deep well cooled the burn until gradually her whole hand felt numb. And in spite of the pain and then the numbness, she was vibrantly aware of the feel of his body... the warmth of solid, muscular chest and lean pelvis and hard thighs. In the rain-spattered window, their image showed his head tilted next to hers in an attitude of care and concern.

Which only goes to show how deceiving images can be, she thought bitterly. "It feels much better now. I don't think the burn is deep." She turned off the water and dried her hand.

"Have you some burn salve or something to put on it? It's in an awkward place that may be hard to heal. You'll probably have to wear gloves for doing dishes and things like that."

"I'll manage."

Determinedly, she walked back to her worktable and picked up the soldering iron again. But the handle of the soldering iron rested exactly on the burned spot. Jordan watched silently as she struggled awkwardly to use the iron at an unfamiliar angle. The thunder was rolling around again, and a couple of times the lights flickered. Once she tensed as the phone gave a tinkle from the bedroom, but the noise was evidently caused by the electrical storm.

"I think I've told you everything I had to say," Barrie said finally. She felt cold... from the rain falling and the chill water running over her hand, and from something else less tangible hovering between them.

He leaned against the worktable, long legs crossed loosely in front of him. "You handled yourself very admirably yesterday. Not everyone would have had the courage and determination to get back on a horse and ride again as you did."

A sharp retort rose to Barrie's lips about Tricia's choice of horse for her, but she managed a stiff "thank you" instead and made no mention of the sore spots that remained from riding in wet clothing. She wished he would go. There were uncomfortable silences, like something unfinished, hanging between them. The night and storm had closed around them, bringing back painful memories of another night, another storm. The brief contact of their bodies in the kitchen had made her all too physically aware of him again.

"How—how is your business going?" Her voice sounded strained and false to her own ears. "It seems I'm always reading about the growing importance and popularity of solar energy."

"I lost a client a few days ago. He looked at my place here and decided he wanted a duplicate on his site. He was very angry when I told him I couldn't do that. But solar homes aren't like conventional homes in that way. You can't yank a design out of one site and plunk it down somewhere else and expect it to work. The microclimate of each site must be considered, as well as its orientation to the sun and physical barriers." There was a brooding look on his face, and his words had a detached, absentminded tone, as if his mind were elsewhere. In an abrupt change of subject, he asked, "When are you going back east?"

The question startled Barrie. She'd thought that entire subject was closed. "I don't know yet. It depends on when Killian can set up an appointment. Mr. Warrenton is out of the country on business right now."

Barrie shivered, as much from nerves as cold. Jordan glanced around and spotted the small electric heater. Before Barrie realized what he was planning to do, he flicked the switch on.

"Don't!" Barrie exclaimed. "It will—" The lights went off.

"—blow a fuse," Jordan finished as they stood there in the total blackness.

Barrie could see absolutely nothing. It was peculiar, but

what her eyes registered was not really darkness but a blinding afterglow of the light. She felt her way to the end of the worktable, mentally calculating where the kitchen door was. "There are some fuses in the—"

They collided, Barrie stumbling off balance in spite of their slow movements. His hand caught her by the shoulder and steadied her. They stood motionless, connected only by that tenuous touch of his hand, but Barrie was tremulously aware of the warm live bulk of his body only inches away. Slowly his hand slid beneath the heavy curtain of her hair and caressed the nape of her neck.

A blue flash of lightning revealed a face in stark contrast to the soft, mesmerizing touch of his hand. His mouth was compressed and hard, the angular jawline almost gaunt. The strange light wiped out the nonessentials and emphasized the rugged bone structure of his face. Barrie tried to draw back, but his hand tightened painfully on her neck.

"I didn't ask you to come over here!" she cried wildly, as if in answer to some unspoken accusation.

"You knew I'd come." He sounded resentful, as if he'd been forced into something against his will. His other hand ran up and down her arm in a gesture that sent an electrifying tingle shooting through her.

The lightning blazed again, illuminating the room with an eerie, otherworldly light. The sharp crack of thunder followed almost instantaneously, indicating the lightning strike had been close, but the sound barely permeated Barrie's consciousness. She was only conscious that Jordan's mouth had found hers, that his arms were crushing her to him. She had the wild, dizzying feeling that the room could dissolve around her and she would neither know nor care. The lightning flashed again, visible even behind her closed eyelids.

Her neck arched backward from the driving pressure of his mouth. He tangled one hand in her hair, supporting her head but punishing her too, as his fingers wound harshly among the darkly glossy strands. Punishing her . . . why? *Why?*

His hoarse words answered her unspoken question, "You make me go half-crazy with wanting you . . ."

The cabin shuddered under the onslaught of the storm—or was it only she who quaked under the onslaught of his kisses? His mouth ravished her throat even as his body forced her back against the table and trapped her there with the hard pressure of his pelvis. The lightning danced around the cabin as if it were the targeted plaything of the gods. The earlier rumbles of the storm had been mere foreplay to the climax raging around them now.

She felt open, boneless, ready to receive all he had to give, and yet something within her protested. No! She would not make love with him on the basis of some stumbled gropings in the dark. There had to be more to it than the accident of physical contact, no matter how incendiary that might be. He wanted her. Every caress of his mouth and hands shouted his desire. But at the same time he seemed angry and resentful, blaming her for making him desire her.

She struggled wildly, throwing her head from side to side to escape the hand tangled in her hair. She lifted her arms and shoved against his broad shoulders, pounded her fists against his chest in helpless fury when her struggles had no effect on him. She had no more control over him than over the storm raging outside.

"It's inevitable," he whispered, his soft voice a contrast to her breathless but silent struggles. "It's been inevitable since—"

A clap of thunder obliterated his words, and he picked her up in his arms. He made his way to the bedroom by the glare of jagged steaks of lightning. He set her down on the bed and fumbled with the buttons of her blouse. Her mind shouted warnings, but it was an impotent little voice, shrill and far away, and no match for the powerful desires flooding through her with tidal force. She wound her arms around his neck, recklessly pulling his mouth down to hers. His patience with the buttons gave out, and an untamed yank sent buttons pinging against walls and floor. With a small groan he dipped his mouth to her breasts.

She tangled her fingers in his hair, holding his head against her, thrusting her aching, eager body toward him. She felt chaotic inside, wanting to give and receive, take and bestow. In the strange bluish light his head dipped lower, his teeth nipping lightly at her belly in a gesture that was at once teasing and ticklish and sensuously tantalizing.

Suddenly he stopped. She sat up, panic-stricken.

"What's wrong?" she cried. Her body suddenly felt lost and desolate without his touch. Then another flash of lightning revealed that he had only straightened up to remove his shirt. His naked chest had a metallic, silvery sheen in the strange light, as if the storm had turned him from human into some pagan statue deifying the male body.

He lay down beside her, hands roaming her, lighting a storm within her to rival nature's display outside. The phone beside the bed tinkled, nature arrogantly cutting in on man's little inventions again. The noise momentarily jerked Barrie back from that wild slide into uncontrolled abandon.

"Jordan, no . . . I don't want to—"

His hand found her most intimate secrets, and the reaction of her body made a lie of her frantically whispered denial of want.

"Not until everything is right between us. Not until you really believe that it's not because I want to see Killian that I'm going back east—"

Jordan raised up on one elbow and reached over to drop the telephone receiver to the floor. He smothered the dial tone with a pillow. "That takes care of Killian," he said huskily.

And, for the moment, it did . . .

The earlier harsh violence of his kisses and caresses softened to a melting sensuousness. He was a tender conquerer who took her to heights she had once despaired of ever reaching again, heights she had sometimes suspected existed only in her fantasies. Heights she knew she could not have reached without the emotion that lifted the wild explosion between them from lust to love.

Afterward they lay with her head resting on his shoulder, her body warm and secure in the protective curve of his arm. She had one arm flung across his chest, one leg tangled with his. She felt as if at long last she was home, where she was always meant to be. At some time during the storm between them, the outside storm had slipped away unnoticed. Now there was only the peace of a gentle rain pattering on the old roof, and a peace swelled within Barrie too.

"I could get up and put a fuse in the box," Jordan said lazily.

Barrie just snuggled closer. She had no need of electricity when she had Jordan.

Barrie slept a sweet, dreamless sleep, rousing only briefly in the morning when Jordan slipped out of bed. He whispered something about having to be at the office for an early appointment, kissed her, and tucked the covers around her.

She didn't wake again until after nine o'clock, far later than she usually slept. She stretched luxuriously, feeling sleek and satisfied as a purring cat. Through the bedroom window she could see a tree near the lake that had been struck by lightning. The trunk was split full length in a raw gash. She had been struck by lightning too, she thought dreamily. Jordan's lightning. But it had not destroyed her; she had been given new life, reborn in love. The bathroom mirror showed an almost outrageous glow on her face.

At ten o'clock Jordan called, laughingly saying that the way she was curled up in bed when he left her had made him think he might catch her still asleep.

"I got lonely and woke up," she said. With brazen suggestiveness she added, "But if you'd like to come out and tuck me in again—"

"Don't tempt me." He laughed, but there was a husky undertone of seriousness.

They made a date to have dinner together Wednesday night. Jordan wanted to take her somewhere nice, but she said she'd rather cook. "The way to a man's heart and all that," she said lightly.

"You already know the way to a man's heart," he shot back meaningfully.

From that moment on, it seemed as if nothing could go wrong with her work. In spite of the burned hand, her fingers flew over the soldering and puttying. The power of love! she thought with a giddy exultance.

Her mind flew too, thinking about the marvelous opportunity to do the restaurant murals, thinking less happily about the inescapable encounter with Killian. She wanted to do the murals, but a trip back east would inevitably again raise a barrier of suspicion and doubt between her and Jordan, a barrier that she felt had at last been lowered.

She argued back and forth with herself. The career-woman part of her insisted she had a right to pursue an important work opportunity, and Jordan should understand and trust her. But the woman-in-love part of her countered that career opportunities would come again. Was grabbing this one worth endangering the new understanding with Jordan?

The basic fact was, given both their inescapable pasts, the trip *would* come between them. And winning Jordan's trust meant more to her than the possibility of winning a commission to do the murals for Mr. Warrenton, no matter how fantastic an opportunity it was. There was no way she could avoid meeting Killian if she went back east. He had made plain that it was his price for setting her up with Warrenton. A price she wasn't willing to pay.

The Wednesday evening dinner was pleasant. Barrie had picked up some pieces of dead wood, and the evening was chill enough for a blaze in the fireplace. They sat together in front of it, Barrie's back against Jordan's chest, his arms and legs curved around her. Jordan didn't talk of any future between them yet, but Barrie was content, serene in the confidence that time would take care of everything now. He planned to drive back to the Portland apartment that evening, but he wound up staying the night, and their lovemaking soared again to star-studded heights. With his parting kiss in the morning, he said he'd see her over the weekend.

The following day, Barrie finally got hold of Killian, whom she'd been unable to reach all week, and told him she had decided against doing the restaurant murals for Mr. Warrenton and not to bother setting up an appointment with him. None too graciously, Killian finally said if she changed her mind to let him know.

Barrie finished the window by midday Friday. She called Vanessa, who was delighted and asked if she could bring it in that day. Barrie explained that the window was so large and heavy she couldn't load it into the car without help.

"However, if Jordan comes out tonight, perhaps I can

get him to help load it and I could have it there tomorrow morning."

"I don't think Jordan is planning to drive out to the lake tonight. He is scheduled to speak at a symposium on solar energy tonight, and Tricia is going to the dinner with him. Well, really, there isn't all that much rush about getting the window here right away." Vanessa laughed her husky, good-natured chuckle, totally unaware that she had dropped a bomb into the midst of Barrie's happiness. "I don't think the workmen can get around to installing it for another week or so. It's just that I'm eager to see it."

Somehow Barrie managed to say that she would find someone else to help her load the window into the car. And she would definitely deliver it the following morning. The effort of keeping her voice casual and unconcerned was so great that her jaws ached by the time she put the phone down.

Jordan had one woman to sleep with in the country . . . and another girl to romance gallantly in the city.

chapter 9

BARRIE CALLED MIKE SETLOW that evening, and he came over to help her load the completed window into her car. She offered to pay him, but he wouldn't hear of it. He stayed around and chatted amiably, confiding that he was rather seriously dating a girl who worked as a maid at Timberline Lodge. If he had any curiosity about the development of her relationship with Jordan, he didn't mention it.

Barrie made every effort to keep her mind blank on that subject, but she spent a restless night. She was on her way to Portland by eight o'clock the following morning. Vanessa had said to bring the window to her home because the office was closed on Saturday.

Barrie located Vanessa's address in an area of stately older homes with sweeping slopes of lawn and magnificent old maples and elms. Vanessa's home was large and elegant, with two immense pillars out front and a railed balcony between them. A windowed cupola was topped with a bronze weatherwane in the shape of a sea bird endlessly scanning the far horizons.

Vanessa was surprised to see Barrie so early. With the gardener's help, they carried the window into the sunny room Vanessa used as an office at home. Vanessa clapped her hands like a delighted child when Barrie unveiled her creation. They discussed the window briefly, and Barrie

complimented Vanessa on her lovely old home. Vanessa
said it had been built by a sea captain in the 1890s. He had
insisted on the cupola so he could watch the ships on the
Columbia. The house had since been remodeled several
times, accounting for what Vanessa laughingly called "an
architectural hodgepodge."

Unexpectedly, Vanessa also extended another invitation.
She was giving a buffet dinner next Saturday night for a
group of people interested in the preservation and renovation
of some of the city's historical structures.

"I'm making it dressy, of course," Vanessa added with
her usual infectious chuckle. "If you make people dress up,
they think whatever cause you're promoting is somehow
more deserving and worthwhile." There would be some real
estate people present, a banker or two, some architects and
builders. She would put Barrie's window on display, and
it would be an excellent opportunity for Barrie to meet
people and make useful contacts.

"Oh, Vanessa, thank you! You've been so kind to me,
but I don't think . . . I mean . . ." Barrie floundered, not
knowing what to say. Didn't Vanessa recognize the strained
triangle linking Barrie and Jordan and Tricia? No, evidently
she did not. Vanessa was so open and aboveboard, such a
thoroughly good-hearted person, that the subtle tensions and
antagonisms and hostilities had passed right by her.

Another cause for hesitation suddenly assailed Barrie,
an uncomfortable guilty feeling that she wasn't playing fair
with Vanessa. Vanessa had been unfailingly kind and hospitable and generous to her . . . and she was intimately involved with the man with whom Vanessa thought her niece
was in love. Would Vanessa be so generously helpful if she
knew about the clandestine relationship between Barrie and
Jordan?

Because clandestine it was, Barrie thought bitterly. Jordan was evidently keeping his nights in her bed a deep, dark
secret.

"Do come," Vanessa urged again as they walked along
the hallway to the foyer.

"You're always doing me favors that I don't seem able

to return," Barrie protested doubtfully.

"I'll pretend you are my own personal discovery and take credit for your marvelous talent." Vanessa, in her generous way, was making it sound as if Barrie would be doing her a favor by coming. In an unexpected change of mood, Vanessa added with a sigh, *"You* might help *me* convince that niece of mine that she ought to go back to college in a couple of weeks."

Barrie concealed her surprise at the uncharacteristically fretful tone of Vanessa's voice. "Does she have other plans?"

"I'm afraid so."

"Concerning Jordan Steele?"

They were in the Persian-carpeted foyer now, and Barrie momentarily wondered where Tricia was at this moment. Sleeping in after a late night out with Jordan?

Vanessa nodded in answer to Barrie's question.

"They evidently see a lot of each other." Barrie's comment was cautious, and she was guiltily aware it was also a small probe for information.

"Perhaps too much." Vanessa sighed again. "I'm afraid I've been seeing their relationship through rose-colored glasses because of my own happy marriage to an older man. But I really think now that Tricia should go back to college for a least one more year. I wouldn't want to see either of them hurt by rushing into something. Tricia is a lovely girl, but still so immature in many ways, more so than most girls her age. And Jordan has those complications from his past."

"I'm afraid none of us can escape our past."

Barrie hadn't realized she sounded so morose until Vanessa gave her a sharp look. "You sound as if you've had a few painful experiences too."

"Oh, a few." Barrie managed to keep her voice light. Vanessa's comments about Jordan and Tricia had lifted Barrie's guilty feeling that her own tenuous relationship with Jordan was somehow a betrayal of Vanessa's friendship. "I'd very much like to come to your dinner Saturday night," she added.

"Good." Vanessa reached over and gave Barrie a warm,

impulsive hug. "I'll count on your youth and beauty to liven up and decorate what might otherwise be a rather stodgy group."

Barrie smiled her thanks at the generous compliment. She left the house with a good feeling, but just as she was getting into her car she glanced back toward the house and caught a flash of movement at a second-story window as a curtain was quickly dropped. She felt certain the hand behind the curtain was Tricia's.

The small gesture abruptly dimmed the pleasant glow that talking with Vanessa had given her. Vanessa might have her doubts about the relationship between Jordan and Tricia, but Barrie knew neither of them were likely to be deterred by someone else's disapproval. What Tricia wanted, Tricia would go after, with all her youthful energy. What Jordan wanted, Jordan would go after with a ruthless determination. And just what *did* Jordan want? When Barrie was in his arms, his passion left no doubt that she was the one he desired. And yet when he was away from her he evidently had some very different thoughts.

Well, that worked two ways, she thought defiantly. Just now she was having some very different thoughts about Jordan than she had when passion overwhelmed her in his arms.

And yet there was one shattering difference, she thought with a certain sense of despair as her defiance drooped. She loved Jordan. *Loved* him.

Barrie drove away from the house with a certain reluctance to return to the lake cabin. Jordan would be at the lake today. He would expect to spend the night with her. She suddenly felt an almost desperate need for both time and space to think, time and space far from the lake and cabin, far from Jordan. In his presence, in his arms, logic and reason seemed to desert her. She was like a compass needle pulled off course by some powerful magnetic force, the magnetic power of Jordan's passion and her love for him.

On sudden impulse she headed not toward the lake but toward the coast, vaguely recalling a few long-ago pleasant excursions to the ocean with her parents. The distance was farther than she had realized, through miles of farm lands and mountainous forests, but she didn't turn back. She let her mind choose its own erratic path, not attempting to figure things out or make decisions, just letting the thoughts dart and flutter where they might. Her head felt almost painfully full of them, like a container filled to the exploding point, and the beginnings of a headache throbbed at her temples.

She smelled and felt the damp sea air before she saw the Pacific itself. She breathed deeply, letting the invigorating air seep into her lungs until each weary cell felt as if it were slowly stirring to fresh life.

A morning fog was just lifting off the coast, and she had the strange, heady feeling that she was seeing some primeval dawn of creation. A rocky headland rose out of a mist . . . translucent green waves topped with froths of white silver crashed on a deserted beach . . . sunlight shimmered through the fog, as if an unseen creator had deemed: *let there be light* . . .

And as the fog dissipated and the sun shone in an astonishingly cloudless sky, there *was* light. The waves sparkled and danced, suddenly more playful than threatening. Barrie parked the car and climbed out on a spray-slickened rock to watch a pair of sea lions. Their sleek bodies rolled gracefully in the turbulent water as they hunted, but sometimes they seemed to forget the seriousness of their task and frolicked in the waves for the sheer joy of it. She lifted her face to sun and wind, letting her mind go blessedly empty.

She drove farther, parked beside a driftwood-strewn beach, and walked and walked until, looking back, her car was only a dot beside the guardrail.

The distance finally seemed to give her thoughts some sense of perspective. Why was she so disturbed? Jordan had taken Tricia to dinner and a meeting. She had stewed that fact around in her mind until it ballooned all out of proportion to its real importance. Put in a simple, unemotional statement—*Jordan had taken Tricia to dinner and a meeting*—the event was reduced in size to the tiny dot of her car in the distance. Jordan had carefully explained his relationship with Tricia. It was a casual, uncomplicated friendship, insignificant next to the passionate feelings that raged between

Barrie and Jordan. She must hold that thought and forget the irrelevant worries and doubts.

Darkness had fallen by the time she got back to her car, but she stood at the guardrail for a moment, eyes closed, letting the wind whip her hair into a dark banner. She felt cleansed, the dark corners of her mind swept clean of clutter and trash. Gone were the imaginary dialogues she had carried on inside her head with Jordan, the scraps of accusation, bits of challenge and threat, spatters of scorn.

She spent the night in a motel within sound of the pounding surf, and next morning ate heavenly light and juicy blueberry hotcakes for breakfast. She bought a pound of succulently rich freshly smoked salmon for Jordan. She walked a pebbly beach and collected pockets full of jewel-bright rocks. Each surge of the waves swirled a fresh selection. It was like strolling in some fabulous jewelry store, with everything free for the taking.

She didn't intend to stay so long, but it was late Sunday night before she returned to the cabin. She felt utterly at peace with herself, Jordan, the world.

She slept dreamlessly, momentarily disoriented when she woke to a shrill, discordant noise that was at odds with her newfound peace. She fumbled for the phone and tried to focus her eyes on the bedside clock at the same time. Six-fifteen? In the *morning?*

"Hello?"

"Where the hell have you been all weekend?"

"Jordan!"

"I've called, and I've been over there, and called some more. If you weren't there this morning, I was ready to contact the police."

Barrie scooted to a cross-legged position on the bed, hearing the anger and worry in Jordan's voice and feeling a guiltily delicious little tingle knowing that he *was* worried. She let him rant and rave for a few moments longer.

"I suppose I should have called and told you," she admitted.

"Told me what?"

"I just felt the need to get away by myself for a little while to think. I went over to the coast and didn't get back until late last night." Her words fell into an absolute silence, a seemingly bottomless void. She shivered, suddenly apprehensive. She rushed on, chattering about the endless beaches, the antics of the sea lions, the quaint shops and towns.

"And all this time you were 'thinking.' did you ever stop to think I might be worried as hell about you?" He didn't give her time to answer. "Obviously not. So what were you thinking about? Killian? Having second thoughts about a reconciliation?"

Barrie was astonished, both by the fury in his voice and his suggestion that she had spent the weekend thinking about *Killian*. It had been Jordan who filled her thoughts. Killian had scarcely entered them.

"I'll never be able to trust you, will I?" He sounded as if he spoke through gritted teeth.

"Perhaps your lack of trust comes because you aren't exactly trustworthy yourself," Barrie snapped back.

"What the hell is that supposed to mean?" His voice was an ominous growl.

"Never mind." She clenched her jaw on the subject of his dinner with Tricia.

"When can I see you?" he demanded abruptly.

"I've been invited to a buffet dinner party at Vanessa's home Saturday evening. No doubt I'll see you there." Barrie slammed the receiver down, her hand clenched around it so tightly her fingers ached when she finally released it.

She threw back the covers. Her robe was on a chair beneath the clothes she had tossed there in carefree abandon the night before. She snatched at the robe and a handful of pebbles spilled out of her jacket pocket as it fell to the floor.

One by one, Barrie slowly picked them up. They were no longer fantastic natural jewels of glowing color. Dry, away from surf and sun, they were merely rounded stones, faded and dull and ordinary.

And her glorious weekend suddenly was also faded and dull and colorless. All the glitter and sparkle were gone. All the crystal-clear insights were shattered into useless splinters. She had lived for a brief time in a never-never land, a fantasy world where everything was clear-cut and uncomplicated. And now she was back to harsh reality.

She tossed the stones into the driveway, and they blended anonymously with the other dull rocks. She plunged into her work, taking time out only for a swim each afternoon. Swimming weather couldn't last much longer. Now her chipmunk friend scurried off to stash whatever she gave him in some secret cache for the winter.

As Saturday approached, Barrie briefly contemplated telephoning Vanessa with some excuse not to attend the dinner party. She discarded the thought before reaching the point of manufacturing some flimsy fib.

Perhaps a bit of pride was involved also, she finally admitted guiltily to herself. She had been hopelessly out of her element at the horse-and-picnic gathering, but she knew how to handle a sophisticated dinner among strangers.

During the week some workmen came and built a boat dock below Jordan's house, and on Saturday morning a moving van arrived. Barrie had heard nothing from him all week after that angry Monday morning call. The appearance of the movers evidently meant he had given up the apartment and would be living full time at the lake now. Barrie resolutely refused to speculate on how that might affect her future . . . if at all.

She dressed carefully but not nervously for the dinner party. No putting on one dress and uncertainly exchanging it for another. And no fade-into-the-wallpaper outfit either. The dress she chose from the extensive wardrobe left over from her Washington social life was silk organza, with a multilayered skirt and a bare back. At first glance, the dress was demure but sophisticated. At second glance, it wasn't quite so demure. The back dipped daringly, and the flutter of the soft ruffle at the bodice and over her shoulders revealed an occasional glimpse of the upper curve of her breasts that was more tantalizing than full exposure. The color was a glowing tangerine that set off the dark sable of her hair and eyes. Slim-heeled sandals and a glitter of teardrop earrings completed her outfit, and she tossed a light evening wrap around her shoulders against the cool of the evening.

The day had settled into dusk as she drove toward Port-

land, though behind her the mountain still glowed in the
sun's last rays. As the dusk deepened, she became aware
of a particular set of headlights that matched her every move.
She passed a semi-truck; so did the headlights. She slowed
behind a sports car behaving erratically; the other car
slowed.

As she parked her car in Vanessa's circular driveway,
the other car pulled around her. The lone occupant flashed
her a coldly dazzling smile. Jordan. She felt her first flutter
of nervousness about the evening and awkwardly scraped
the tires against the low brick curb bordering the drive.

Jordan was waiting as she slid out of her car. Nervous
excitement heightened her already dramatic coloring and
brought a dark sparkle to her eyes. She could feel Jordan's
glance flick over her, but his reaction was impossible to
read against the backdrop of the house, dramatically illu-
minated by outdoor lights. He was wearing an impeccably
cut dinner jacket and black tie. He looked darkly, if somehow recklessly, handsome. Barrie felt another twinge of
nervousness.

"It seems a shame we brought two cars when one would
have been sufficient." Unasked, Jordan cupped her elbow
with his hand as they started up the steps. She gritted her
teeth against an instantaneous but unwanted reaction to his
touch. "We're not doing our part to conserve energy."

"If we enter the house together, people will assume we
came together anyway."

"Does that disturb you?"

"Of course not. Does it disturb you?" she challenged in
return.

"Of course not." His echo was mocking.

But will it disturb Tricia, Barrie wondered wryly.

Tricia, however, was not around to see them enter together. Barrie was uncertain whether she was relieved or
disappointed.

"Barrie, you look good enough to eat!" Vanessa greeted
gaily. Vanessa herself looked quite stunning in a blue-gray
chiffon that swirled in a misty cloud around her.

Barrie accepted a glass of white wine and peered cautiously around the living room. Where was Tricia? Was it

possible she had decided to skip the dinner party as too dull and stodgy? The living room was done with white French antique furniture, elegant but not fussy, and ice-blue carpet. Displayed on artist's easels were photographs of various structures proposed for preservation or already restored. Barrie did not, however, see her window anywhere. Had Vanessa decided against displaying it, after all?

Vanessa, quite without guile, Barrie was sure, separated Barrie and Jordan. Barrie found herself in a group discussing an old bank building that a developer was tearing down, although she was quickly aware that she was as much an object of interest as was the bank building. Out of the corner of her eye she kept track of Jordan. At the moment he was bent over, listening attentively to something a petite elderly woman in silver satin was saying.

At that moment Tricia made her entrance. There was no fanfare of drums, no announcement, and yet practically every head turned to look at her as she paused in the doorway for effect. Her golden hair was swept into a seductive bedroom tousle of curls and tendrils. She was wearing pleated black chiffon evening pants, a barely-there camisole, also black and embroidered in metallic gold, and gold sandals with spike heels so high she seemed in danger of losing her balance. Only the pleats kept the outfit from being totally transparent, and Barrie doubted that the girl wore anything beneath the camisole.

As if a signal had been given, people suddenly realized they were staring and returned to their conversations. Tricia looked just a trifle risqué for a gathering such as this, Barrie thought as the girl strolled across the room with hips swinging almost recklessly, considering the height of the spike heels. But she ruefully had to admit that perhaps her opinion had a tinge of sour grapes. Tricia was stunning, no doubt about it.

Barrie shot a quick glance at Jordan. His mouth had literally dropped open. Tricia headed straight toward him, the black chiffon evening pants swirling seductively around her slim legs.

With an effort, Barrie forced her attention back to the conversation around her. Somehow she managed to make an appropriate murmur or ask a pertinent question now and then. She felt a growing certainty that Tricia had decided a horsey picnic wasn't the only place she could outshine Barrie, and from the look on Jordan's face, Tricia was well on her way to another triumph.

One man, however, seemed to have eyes only for Barrie. She supposed she should be flattered. He was the second most attractive man in the room. But she really didn't feel like making flirtatious small talk, and she could tell by the gleam in his eyes that he had something on his mind besides the preservation of historical buildings. He introduced himself as Brad Rayburn and said he was a real estate broker. He inquired about where she lived and how long she had been in Oregon and where she worked. All very innocuous, but his eyes sent such a smoldering message that she was tempted to ask if he practiced the look in front of a mirror. He was definitely on the prowl.

"I never expected to find anyone like you here tonight," he said, barely letting her finish saying she had her own business working with stained glass. "And to think I almost didn't come. Do you believe in fate?" His voice was deliberately husky.

Sometimes I believe in fate, Barrie thought to herself. But she didn't believe in tired old preproposition lines even when they were spoken by a physically attractive man. She could have mouthed his next line of dialogue even before he spoke it.

"What do you say we get out of here?"

"And go where?" She was mildly curious about just how outrageous his suggestion would be.

"Dancing? Though I'd really prefer someplace where we could talk and get to know each other better."

"That would be your apartment." Barrie intended to follow through with a quick "no, thanks" and politely excuse herself, but just at that moment Brad Rayburn was cornered by an older man who wanted to talk about selling an apartment building. It seemed the ideal time to make her escape, but Brad Rayburn's arm slipped possessively around her waist. Unless she wanted to make an issue of it, she was trapped.

Her eyes roamed the room as the two men talked. Vanessa was here and there and everywhere, guiding people together, subtly separating and stirring them. Tricia, standing in front of an artist's easel with her hands clasped behind her back, was making a pretense of studying a photograph. For just a moment she looked like a disconsolate child dressed in grown-up clothes, but then Jordan returned with a drink for her and the smile she flashed him was definitely not childish.

Suddenly Barrie became aware of something else. Brad Rayburn had planted his hand in the middle of the lowest point of her bare back, and his fingers were stealthily but inexorably creeping beneath the silk material. Given a few more moments, he'd have the curve of her derriere cupped in his hand.

Barrie glanced up at him in furious outrage. His smooth conversation about the apartment building never wavered, and his hand continued its exploration. Everyone could see—

No, no one could see, Barrie realized. Rayburn was too slick for that. She was backed almost into a corner and only she—and he—knew what was going on. He deserved a sharp palm across the face, but she couldn't do that without making a shocking scene and she didn't want to do that at Vanessa's party. She stood the indignity a moment longer.

"Excuse me, but—" Barrie smiled winningly at the older man who owned the apartment building and stood on tiptoe to murmur into Brad Rayburn's ear. "Mr. Rayburn, I'm going to whisper this the first time. Please remove your hand from my buttock." She kept a sweet smile on her face as she used the deliberately blunt word. "If you don't comply immediately, I'm going to repeat the request. Very loudly."

Brad Rayburn gave her a shocked look, as if she were the one taking indecent liberties, but he pulled his hand away. Barrie murmured excuses and slipped away, and no one else was aware of what had happened. He'd been easy, she thought, compared to some of the persistent "feelers" she'd coped with in Washington. And there she'd sometimes had the furious feeling Killian would prefer she'd let them feel, if it would help his political career.

The next time Barrie spotted Brad Rayburn, he had zeroed in on Tricia, and she appeared to be lapping up his every word. Where was Jordan?

A few minutes later dinner was announced and the double doors to the dining room thrown open. Barrie forgot everything else as she saw what Vanessa had done. Mounted on the far wall above the buffet table was her Mt. Hood window. It was displayed to perfection, with just the proper amount of diffused light behind it and an elegant frame to set it off. There were audible murmurs of appreciation.

Vanessa was suddenly there to give her a quick hug. "Do you like it?"

"You've made it look like a—a work of art!" Barrie said breathlessly.

Vanessa waved an arm for attention. She introduced Barrie with a little speech that wasn't quite a commercial but hinted that her talents were available. Several people stopped by to offer compliments on their way to the table.

The buffet table was almost a work of art, too. Tall silver candlesticks flanked an enormous baked salmon and a variety of other dishes. Barrie filled her plate and found a seat on a wicker chair in the less formal family room which had also been opened up. Her heart thudded as Jordan unexpectedly pulled up a chair beside her.

"The window looks even more spectacular than I expected from what I had already seen of it."

"Thank you. Vanessa did a lovely job of displaying it."

They each took a few bites in silence. Had Jordan sought her out or had this seating arrangement come by chance?

"The movers transferred everything out to the house today. I'll be living there full time now."

Barrie murmured, "Yes, I saw the moving van," and then wished she hadn't said it. It sounded as if she'd been standing there watching with breathless anticipation.

"I wish you had told me you were going to the coast." His voice was low, as if it were an effort to control his anger.

Barrie had the feeling the brief preceding conversation

had been merely a required preliminary to the main event. She took a deep breath. "I don't think this is the place to argue about—"

"Are we arguing?" He gave her that dazzling but icy smile again. "I merely made a comment."

Barrie hesitated and finally said, "It was a rather impulsive decision." She pushed a chunk of baked salmon around on the plate in a pretense of eating. She was suddenly reminded that the smoked salmon she had lovingly purchased for Jordan was languishing in the freezer compartment of her refrigerator. "I don't think it was enough to warrant your judging me untrustworthy."

Before Jordan could say anything, a middle-aged woman descended on them, almost ecstatic in her praise of Barrie's work. She had an antique window which had come out of her grandparents' home, and she wanted Barrie to restore it for her.

As the woman chattered on, Barrie was aware that Jordan kept glancing beyond her into the other room. Finally he excused himself. Barrie groaned inwardly. She was pleased with the possibility of doing the restoration work. Contacts such as this were her reason for being here. But why did the woman have to interrupt just *now*? Barrie managed to twist casually in her chair so she could look into the other room. Jordan was now standing like a thundercloud between Tricia and Brad Rayburn. Even after the woman wandered away from Barrie, Jordan didn't return. He stuck to Tricia as if an invisible string attached them. A waiter finally came and removed Jordan's plate of half-eaten food.

A man stopped by to discuss a larger project, a series of individual entryway panels for a line of custom homes he was building. From a business standpoint this dinner had definitely been worthwhile, but Barrie felt restless. It was a little early to leave, but she didn't think she could take much more of watching Jordan hover over Tricia. Impulsively she decided to go up to the cupola to see the view. Vanessa had announced earlier that it was open for anyone who was interested. Glancing back as she left the room, she saw Jordan's gaze flick her way. She resisted an impulse to make some childish gesture of defiance at him.

It was a steep two-story climb to the cupola, and Barrie felt a little breathless as she stepped into the small, faceted room. But the view was worth the effort. The city was a panorama of brilliant jewels, the distant bridges streams of light arching over the broad, dark emptiness of the Columbia River.

A moment later Barrie heard footfalls on the carpeted stairway. Jordan had seen her head this direction. She braced herself for an inevitable clash between them, but there was an undeniable quiver of expectancy in her body as she whirled to meet him.

"Tricia!"

Barrie's surprised gasp held both dismay and disappointment, but Tricia didn't seem to notice. She moved from window to window, arms hugged around herself. Her color was high, the pupils of her eyes dilated to brilliant, bottomless pools, but Barrie doubted that it was an artificial high induced by liquor or drugs. It was a natural high of being young and beautiful and desirable.

Barrie leaned back against a window ledge. "Where's your friend Brad?"

"Jordan told him to stop annoying me."

"You didn't look annoyed."

Tricia just shrugged her bare shoulders. She was looking out a window, but she was seeing something far more marvelous inside her head. Suddenly she stopped and focused on Barrie.

"You're having an affair with Jordan, aren't you?"

Barrie was so astonished by the blunt but almost casually spoken statement that she neither denied nor agreed with it.

"Aunt Van doesn't know, of course. She's such a simple, trusting innocent—"

The scorn in Tricia's voice toward the woman who had been so good to Barrie prompted an immediate and angry reaction. "Your aunt is one of the sweetest, most caring, good-hearted—"

"That's beside the point." Tricia waved a hand in airy

dismissal. "The point is, you and Jordan are carrying on an affair. It's in the way he looks at you, as if he knows every inch of you."

Barrie felt incriminating color flood her face. This time her silence, neither admitting nor denying, was deliberate. Then, quite simply, she said, "I love him."

"That is unfortunate." Tricia sounded coolly unconcerned. "Because I know, whether you do or not, that the affair means nothing except that Jordan is a virile man with normal male needs. But he's never going to marry you, if that's what you're waiting and hoping for." Seeing the look on Barrie's face, Tricia stabbed deeper. "He's never mentioned marriage to you, has he?"

"Do you think he's going to marry *you?*" The biting words came out of the pain of Barrie's private knowledge that Jordan hadn't mentioned marriage. Blindly, she struck out again. "He's told me you're like a kid sister to him. Just someone fun and uncomplicated—"

"But I have one advantage you lost a long time ago." Tricia's voice was arch. "My . . . innocence."

Barrie repeated the word blankly. "Innocence?"

"I'm a virgin." Tricia spoke as if she were explaining something to a simpleminded child, and Barrie had the momentary wild feeling that Tricia was going to go on and elaborate further, as if the state were somehow beyond Barrie's comprehension.

Barrie took a steadying breath. This conversation was preposterous. "I doubt that Jordan is prudish enough to consider that status a woman's most priceless asset."

"Perhaps not. But it means something more to Jordan. It means I have no past. No former lover, no former husband to complicate things." She smiled. "Jordan may be sleeping with you now, but he'll *marry* me."

"He thinks you're nothing but a child!"

It was a desperate, last-ditch defense and merely brought a smile to Tricia's mouth. She struck a deliberately provocative pose with shoulders back and high, young breasts outthrust, one hip tilted seductively. There was no need for words. After tonight Jordan would never see Tricia as merely a child. She looked all woman, from the tendrils of her tousled hair to the slim heels of her golden shoes.

"We both know all about Jordan's past," Tricia went on conversationally. "His first wife left him to go back to her old love. The second girl he loved went back to her husband. After those experiences, do you really think he'd consider marrying another woman with a past?"

Some detached corner of Barrie's mind noted that Tricia, like Vanessa, didn't realize that Barrie herself was that second girl who had betrayed Jordan's love. She just stood there staring at Tricia, wild protests shooting through her mind but no words coming from her mouth. None would come . . . because with sudden, stunning clarity Barrie knew that Tricia was right. Vanessa's earlier revelations about Jordan's past had given Barrie a sympathetic understanding of his persistent doubts and suspicions, but it had taken Tricia's smug complacency to stab home the agonizing truth that there was no way Barrie could overcome the past, his or hers. She had been deceiving herself, living in a fantasy world, to think time and understanding could change anything.

Jordan might feel a wild sexual passion for her, a passion she had desperately wanted to believe was love. But a blazing affair was one thing to Jordan and marriage quite another. The experiences of the past had hardened his heart until it was as cold and unyielding as the sound of his name, until it was like steel.

Now Barrie understood what Jordan had meant when he called Tricia uncomplicated, though perhaps he didn't fully realize it himself just yet. It meant more than her fresh young body and personality; it meant there were no complications from her past, no entanglements. No ghosts lurked behind her, only the promise of a golden future. Before tonight he had dismissed Tricia as a child, but now she was woman. Barrie herself had seen that revelation dawn on his face.

Tricia had all that to offer him . . . youth and beauty, untarnished past and shining future . . . and Barrie had only her love to give.

With a small, mute gasp of agony, Barrie turned and fled down the winding stairs.

chapter 10

SOMEHOW BARRIE MANAGED to stop and murmur a few polite words to Vanessa. She was thankful that two other couples were leaving at the same time, and in the minor confusion she didn't have to explain her rather abrupt departure. She grabbed her evening wrap and hurried out to the car.

Outside, the lights illuminating the house seemed almost painfully brilliant, each one a starburst design seen through the glaze of tears in her eyes. She stabbed ineffectually at the keyhole several times before finally managing to unlock the car door. She started the engine, ground the gears, and felt an instant flood of nervous perspiration as she tried to maneuver the car out of the tight parking space. She glanced in the rear-view mirror and saw a shadow of movement. Jordan? The thought suddenly panicked her, and her foot pressed harder on the gas pedal than she intended. A sickening crunch reverberated around and through her as the car jarred to a standstill.

Slowly, dazed, she got out and looked at the damage. The right rear wheel had run up on the brick curb and the fender had smashed into a metal pole holding a coach lantern. The pole was now tilted at a crazy angle. The crash was as noisy as it had seemed from within the car, and several people came running down the steps.

"Barrie, are you all right?" Vanessa gasped as her arm circled Barrie's shoulders.

"Look what I've done!" Barrie simply stood there, staring helplessly at the crushed fender with the light pole angling out of it like some strange growth. Her mind seemed to have stopped functioning.

Jordan arrived then, his commanding figure opening an instant pathway through the small crowd of people milling around. His eyes gave Barrie an instant appraisal. "You're not hurt?"

"No. I—I'm fine." She clasped her hands together to keep them from trembling.

Jordan slid behind the steering wheel and managed to jolt the car away from the pole, but the right rear wheel skidded rather than rolled. The metal fender was jammed into the tire, and the tire was already going flat. Jordan got out and inspected the damage briefly.

"You won't be able to drive the car until the fender is straightened."

"There's nothing that can be done about it tonight. Barrie, you're shivering!" Vanessa put her arm around Barrie again. "Come back inside. You can stay here at the house tonight and we'll worry about the car tomorrow."

"No!" A sudden larger-than-life image of Tricia exploded in Barrie's mind. She couldn't stay under the same roof with Tricia, couldn't face her knowing looks in the morning. Barrie's vehement protest drew curious glances, and she felt as if she were standing vulnerably exposed in some blinding spotlight. "I mean, I—I'd just rather go home."

"I can drive her out to the lake." Jordan's authoritative voice spoke to Vanessa rather than to Barrie herself.

"But, Jordan, you promised you'd stay here tonight." Tricia's petulant voice was almost a wail. She had followed the others out of the house. With the brilliantly lit house behind her, every curve of her body was visible through the filmy material of her outfit.

Barrie looked in dismay from the girl to the damaged car and then to Jordan. She didn't want to stay here, but she certainly did not want to ride home with Jordan either. And yet she couldn't just stand there rejecting everything. She had to make some kind of decision. She postponed it by saying vaguely, "I'll contact my insurance company about fixing the light pole."

"Don't worry about it." Vanessa's voice was firm and reassuring.

Jordan abruptly made the decision Barrie was evading. "I'll get my car."

The brief excitement over, the milling group dispersed. Barrie reluctantly slid into Jordan's car when he backed it around the curve of the driveway.

They drove in silence until they were out of the city. Barrie kept her evening wrap clutched around her, as if it might shield her from something unpleasant she knew was coming.

Finally Jordan glanced at her. "What happened? You're a better driver than that."

She would never tell him about that stunning encounter with Tricia. "I just didn't see the light pole," she murmured evasively.

He reached over and switched on the radio, impatiently twisting the dial until he found quiet music on an FM station. "This does give us a chance to continue our earlier interrupted conversation."

Barrie gazed out the side window and remained silent.

"Do you know what I thought when I couldn't find you all weekend?" He didn't give her time to answer before he went on bitterly. "I thought you'd done what you did before. I thought there had been another 'big emergency' and you'd picked up and run back to Killian again." His tone made a mockery of the words *big emergency*.

Barrie turned startled eyes to him. It had never occurred to her he would think that. Then anger replaced her surprise. "Jordan, I have told you repeatedly—"

"So when are you going back east? For your business meeting, of course." He put another sarcastic inflection on *business meeting*, as if he still didn't believe that was the real reason for her planned trip.

"I'd rather not discuss it." She kept her face turned to the window.

"Why?"

Why? Because she had given up the fantastic opportunity for him, because she loved him and hadn't wanted anything to come between them. But pride kept her from telling him that now. It was too much like begging or bargaining for his love. It was too much like saying, *I made this enormous sacrifice for you, and now you owe me your love.*

The truth was, she'd do anything for him. Make any sacrifice. Mold the future to suit him. But she was helpless to change the barrier of the past that stood between them, helpless to erase the shadows it cast over the future. She couldn't bring back the innocence Tricia flaunted, either emotionally or physically.

But all she said was a flat, "That's my business."

More silence. A layer of clouds hung around the base of the mountain, but the peak gleamed in the night sky, timelessly unchanged while everything seemed to be crumbling around Barrie.

"I'm sorry if bringing me home interrupted other plans you'd made," she said finally.

He shrugged. "It was nothing important."

Plans with Tricia unimportant? Barrie felt a small flicker of surprise. "Tricia looked very beautiful tonight," she ventured. "Very . . . mature." Barrie's comment was phrased as a statement, but in reality it was a question, a very vital question. And a moment later she had her answer.

"Yes. She looked very grown-up." A frown line formed between his eyes. "Very lovely."

"Brad Rayburn noticed that too."

Jordan shot a scowl in Barrie's direction. "After you gave him the brush-off. I saw him trying to get his hands on you. I don't know what you said or did to him, but it was evidently effective." The hint of a smile played momentarily around his mouth, as if the thought gave him a certain satisfaction. Then his lips tightened. "Tricia hasn't the experience to know how to handle a man like Rayburn."

Barrie couldn't hold back a taunt. "She appeared to me to be rather enjoying his attentions."

"Rayburn is an ass." He paused, and a muscle jerked along his jawline. "Unfortunately, his smooth line seems to be effective on a certain number of women. I didn't want Tricia to be foolish enough to fall for it."

"Did it ever occur to you she might have been trying to make you jealous?"

She saw his hands tighten on the steering wheel. "The thought occurred to me."

A dangerous game, Barrie thought, given Jordan's past. And yet it had evidently worked. Yes, Tricia had accomplished much tonight, Barrie thought unhappily. She had forced Jordan finally to see her as a woman. She had let him see that other men found her attractive. And then she had sweetly and demurely accepted his protection, still innocently untouched, making plain he was the only one who really mattered.

Tricia might be inexperienced, Barrie thought grimly, but she had a feminine instinct that was sharp and ready as a switchblade.

They drove in silence, finally rattling over the rough road past the campground where camp fires still glowed like flickering golden eyes in the night. When the car stopped, Barrie instantly reached for the door handle. His hand on her arm stopped her. She looked over at him, lips parted.

His mouth asked a simple question. "What do you want to do about your car?" But his eyes asked something more, and his fingers made a softly sensuous movement against her arm.

No! she thought in wild defiance. She would not make love with him tonight, now when she knew it meant no more to him than mere sexual need. Not even though she felt a tongue of fire start at his hand and race through her . . .

"I don't think I can get hold of my insurance company until Monday." Her voice sounded thick and stiff to her own ears.

"I can arrange to have the car towed in and repaired, if you like."

"Thank you." She fumbled with the door again and fled. At the cabin door, in the glare of the headlights, she fumbled frantically in her purse for the key. A shadow crossed the headlights. She looked back at him with a kind of terror on her face. "No! You can't—"

"You dropped your evening wrap. I was just bringing it to you."

Gently he slid the soft cashmere around her shoulders. His hands came with it, and he held her arms lightly from behind as his head dipped to touch his lips to the soft curve of her neck.

She stood there, eyes closed, fighting him, fighting herself. Echoes of Tricia's smug words assaulted her. "He may be sleeping with you, but he'll *marry* me." His hands slid down to mold her hips, to press her body back against the hard masculine lines of his. His mouth did wild things to her throat, and an electric shiver tingled through her as his lips nibbled her earlobe.

"You were the most beautiful woman there tonight," he murmured huskily. "Every time I looked across the room at you, I wanted to take you in my arms."

But you didn't. You stayed right by Tricia, let me battle Rayburn on my own.

"I'm sorry about your car, but I'm glad I had an excuse to bring you home . . ." His hand slid beneath the flirty ruffle of her dress and cupped her breast with exquisite tenderness.

He doesn't love you . . . he only wants you . . .

The voices of reason and logic and warning churned through her. "No . . ." she whispered helplessly as he turned her to face him. His mouth found hers, came down with a hard, demanding hunger that forced an opening through her crumbling defenses as commandingly as he had forced a pathway through the milling people.

"I want to make love to you . . ."

Not *I love you*. Not *marry me*. And yet if this was all she could have of him, why not take it? If this was all that could ever be, why not seize it?

Her passive mouth turned wild and reckless under his, and she lifted her arms to hold his head fiercely. Take what there was. . . . She met the probe of his tongue with her own, pressed the swelling fullness of her breasts against his chest and felt the answering pressure of his male desires.

And maybe, just maybe, by some miracle, this wouldn't be all there was . . .

Later, much later, as she lay beside his slumbering form, her body languid and satiated but her mind roaming restlessly, she was to ask herself: how many women in love had deceived themselves with that very same hope? Miracles didn't happen.

But she had chosen her irrevocable course. She would give him her love, take what he had to offer, for as long . . . or as short . . . a time as it might last.

In the morning, they went over to Jordan's house. The movers had placed the furniture in approximately the correct positions in the various rooms, but boxes of kitchen supplies and food were merely stacked on counters and against walls. They managed to give the kitchen some semblance of order, then went upstairs to tackle boxes of linens and clothing.

But instead they wound up making love on the king-size bed, and to Barrie's dreamy eyes the rainbow reflections of light through the stained-glass skylight seemed the physical image of what she felt inside when they made love. If she could paint a picture of how the ecstasy felt, that would be it . . . shimmers and ripples and ribbons of vibrant, glorious color. And yet she had a strangely bittersweet, lastdays feeling even as she lay warm and satisfied in the tangle of Jordan's arms and legs. A feeling akin to the time as a child she walked out on the high-dive board for the first time and saw the yawning emptiness beyond.

Suddenly the doorbell chimed. Beside her on the enormous bed Jordan, startled, raised up on one elbow. "Who can *that* be?"

Barrie leaned over and planted a kiss on his hard, flat belly. She had always wanted to do that. And now, almost as if it were the last chance she would ever have, she had done it. He tasted warm, a little salty. He grinned and walked naked to the window while the doorbell chimed again.

"Good Lord," he groaned. "There's a whole mob out there."

Jordan yelled that he was coming, and then they scrambled around trying to find their clothes and dress themselves and straighten the bed all at once. Jordan went downstairs and Barrie went into the bathroom and made a pretense of stocking the mirrored cabinet. She doubted that all their scurrying around was going to fool anyone, however. The bathroom mirror showed the reflection of a woman to whom a man had just made passionate love. Her mouth had a well-kissed, voluptuous fullness, and her eyes a heavy-lidded bedroom look. Even her hair, in spite of a quick combing, looked as if it had just been tousled on a pillow.

But when she heard Tricia's voice downstairs, she felt a certain grim satisfaction that she looked exactly as she did.

She went downstairs carrying an armload of towels to give her presence upstairs some credibility.

"Barrie just came over to give me a hand straightening out this mess." Jordan sounded a little too hearty. He waved a hand vaguely around the living room. The room was in perfect order.

Tricia's blue eyes regarded Barrie venomously. Barrie suspected Tricia's attitude toward Jordan's affair and "male needs" might not be quite so tolerant after this close contact with the intimate details.

"We just came out to give Jordan an impromptu house-warming," Vanessa said gaily. "There was all this food left over from last night, and it seemed the perfect excuse to descend on him and make use of his new dock and boat."

Between Vanessa and Jordan, Barrie was introduced to everyone, though not all the names stuck. There was Jordan's partner in the architectural firm, Bill Andrews, and his wife and children, an older couple Barrie remembered from last night, plus several other young couples with children.

"We're not very well organized," Vanessa confessed cheerfully, "since this was all spur-of-the-moment, but we do want to wish you the very best in your new home." She handed Jordan a package which turned out to be an enormous chef's apron and hat for barbecuing. "That's a hint that we expect to be invited out often for barbecues and swims."

It was a casual, jovial group. Vanessa was more relaxed than she had been at last night's purposeful party. The kids were in the water within minutes and the adults soon afterward. Tricia changed to a seductively draped blue bikini. Again there was nothing even remotely childish about her lithe but curvaceous figure. Tricia was not, however, Barrie realized in surprise, a particularly good swimmer. Her dives from the dock made almost cannonball splashes, and she didn't kick properly. But she seemed to be having fun splashing around, and she looked so delicious in the frothy bit of bathing suit that Barrie doubted if anyone noticed her lack of swimming skill.

Jordan took the kids out in the boat, two or three at a time. He was wearing leopard-spotted swim trunks and looked almost primitively male in spite of the domestic activities with the children, which he seemed to be enjoying thoroughly. Finally he relinquished the job to one of the fathers, swam with Tricia for a few minutes, and then, dripping puddles of water, dropped down beside Barrie.

"Don't you want to swim?"

"I didn't bring a suit along."

"Why don't you go over and get it? I could run you over in the boat."

"No. Let the kids enjoy the boat."

"Well, suit yourself." He sounded unconcerned. He was watching Tricia pose on the dock, sitting with her arms behind her and head thrown back to accentuate every curve of her body.

"But I might take the car and drive over and get my suit, if you wouldn't mind."

"No, of course not. The keys are in the car."

At the cabin, Barrie changed, then slipped her jeans and shirt on over the swimsuit. She combed her hair, straightened the love-tangled bed, hunted for a different pair of sandals. Finally she had to admit to herself that she was dawdling, reluctant to go back across the lake.

Why?

Because she was afraid she couldn't compete with Tricia? Afraid Tricia would score another triumph as she had at both the picnic and dinner party? Yes.

But if there was one area in which she *could* outshine Tricia, Barrie thought grimly as she remembered the girl's awkward dives, it was in the water. Recklessly she changed to a different swimsuit, a bikini she seldom wore because it was so skimpy.

Quickly she drove back around the lake. Jordan and Tricia were sitting on the wooden-planked dock, their feet dangling in the water. Barrie stripped off her jeans and shirt and dropped them on a webbed lounge chair. She walked down the zig-zag trail to the dock, kicked off her sandals, and made a clean, almost noiseless dive into the cold water. When she surfaced some distance out, both Jordan and Tricia were watching her. Tricia's mouth was turned down at the corners in a small, displeased frown. Barrie swam back to the dock in a graceful breaststroke. The water-level dock, with no spring to it, was an awkward place from which to dive, but Barrie managed a fairly respectable pike dive. She backstroked to the dock, aware of a deepening pout on Tricia's face. Barrie's expertise in the water was obviously an unpleasant surprise to her.

Jordan already knew of Barrie's swimming abilities, of course. He had seen her in the water. But he hadn't seen her dive before, and his expression was openly admiring, which gave Barrie a small sense of satisfaction.

"Maybe I'll have to add a diving board to the dock," he called as she poised for another dive.

"And maybe she ought to give the rest of us lessons." Jordan's partner, Bill Andrews, had strolled down to the dock and was also watching admiringly. He was a pleasant guy, but considerably softer bodied than Jordan. His somewhat overweight wife, just starting down the trail, called some cheerfully teasing comment about how they both swam like a couple of beached whales.

Barrie dove again, but at the same moment Tricia suddenly shoved Jordan off the dock. He grabbed her foot and jerked her under too. When they came up, they both splashed the couple standing on the dock. A moment later all four were roughhousing in the water, squealing and splashing, ducking and laughing. Barrie was forgotten.

So much for trying to outshine Tricia, Barrie thought wryly as she watched the exuberant horseplay. As usual, Tricia had managed to turn all attention, and particularly

Jordan's attention, to herself.

Barrie treaded water for a few moments, feeling like an outsider looking in on the fun. She should have stayed at the cabin, she thought unhappily. She should never have come back over here. She didn't belong. She fought back tears of hurt and frustration. She couldn't go back to the dock crying...

She whirled in the water and with a hard crawl stroke headed for the center of the lake. Perhaps she would just keep on going, she thought wildly. Swim all the way across the lake to the cabin and not come back at all. And probably no one would even miss her, she thought unhappily, least of all Jordan.

The vigorous swim, as usual, cleared her head of such thoughts. She couldn't just run off like some petulant child, she realized ruefully, angry because no one was playing with her. She slowed her steady stroke and decided to turn back. She was past the mid center of the lake now, not tired, but with the fresh edge worked off her energy.

Barrie wasn't aware until she turned that someone else was in the water, not as far out as she was, but a long distance from shore. Barrie watched curiously, unable to identify the splashing figure. Jordan? She didn't think so. If he had wanted to swim with her he'd have called for her to wait or simply overtaken her. It wasn't necessarily even someone from the housewarming party, she decided. There were other groups swimming nearby, though few people ventured as far out as the splashing figure.

Whoever it was, Barrie realized with growing alarm, had no business venturing that far from shore. The swimmer was not an expert by any means. The person was doing a lot of kicking and splashing but making very little forward progress.

Barrie cupped a hand around her mouth. "Turn around! You're getting too far out!"

And then, before her horrified eyes, the figure floundered and sank. The water roiled and bubbled from the frantic disturbance below. The figure surfaced, flailing wildly, and let out a shrill scream of terror.

Tricia!

Barrie flattened her body to a hard racing stroke and sprinted toward the girl. The distance seemed endless. The usually friendly water had become her enemy, dragging at her body and holding her back.

My God, what was Tricia doing out here? How had she gotten so far from shore without someone stopping her? Why had she ventured so far out? Tricia was screaming, sinking, thrashing to the surface, using up what little strength she had left.

Barrie let up for just a moment to scream at the girl. "Don't struggle! Let yourself float!"

But the girl was beyond following any instructions, perhaps beyond hearing them. She was obviously growing weaker, and her shrieks ended in gagging coughs.

"Take it easy," Barrie called as she got closer. She could see the pure terror on Tricia's contorted face now. "I'm coming."

Barrie was no more than two strokes from Tricia when the girl sank, the sun-kissed blond hair floating on the surface for a moment and then drifting downward with a laziness that belied the horror of the moment.

Barried didn't hesitate. She took a deep breath and dove, thankful that in the translucent water she could see the girl's limp, spread-eagled form plainly. She got a grip on the girl and used a powerful kick to propel them both to the surface.

She automatically tossed her head to flip the hair out of her face and suck in a quick breath of air the moment she surfaced. Tricia's body was a sagging, dead weight, her head flopping limply. Barrie took a split moment to orient herself with the shoreline. There was no point wasting time trying to attract attention with screams or waves. Surely people on shore had heard and seen what was happening. If they hadn't, they weren't likely to notice anything Barrie might do now.

Barrie momentarily relaxed her grip as she tried to get a better hold on Tricia for the ordeal ahead. Barrie had had a little lifesaving training, but she had never actually pulled a drowning person in. The distance looked endless. And just at that moment the unexpected happened. Barrie thought the girl was unconscious, but suddenly she exploded in manic terror. Her arms flailed air and water like a windmill gone berserk. She gasped and choked for breath, flinging her head from side to side in a frenzy. Barrie reeled as a blow caught her on the temple, and she choked and swallowed water.

"Tricia!" she gasped, fighting the girl's clawing hands. "Stop—"

But now it was Tricia who had a hold on Barrie, a hold coupled with a strength born of panic and terror. She was trying to climb on top of Barrie, use her as a ladder to safety. Her knee hit Barrie in a stunning blow to her chest, and her clawing fingernails raked Barrie's mouth and eyes. She got a knee on Barrie's shoulder, and Barrie felt herself floundering, sinking beneath the weight.

Suddenly it wasn't just a struggle to save Tricia's life, it was a frantic battle to save her own too. Tricia was everywhere, on her, over her, clawing and scratching and climbing. Barrie's lungs were bursting as Tricia's frantic attempt to climb on her kept her beneath the water.

Tricia was behind her now, both arms locked around Barrie's head in a frantic effort to keep her own face above water. One arm choked Barrie's throat, the other was wrapped around her eyes, blinding her. With a reeling sense of dizziness, Barrie felt her own consciousness beginning to fade . . .

chapter 11

BARRIE CLAWED WEAKLY at the arms that imprisoned her with the superhuman strength born of terror. She reached up and tried to grab Tricia's hair, but it floated somewhere out of reach. Her frantic struggles to kick to the surface weakened, and her legs dangled limply. She felt herself sinking . . . down, down, down . . .

There was a frenzied scrabbling movement above her as Tricia's head sank below the surface too. The grip covering Barrie's eyes slipped sideways, and the sudden glimpse of something other than terrorizing darkness gave her a momentary burst of strength. She grabbed Tricia's wrist with one hand and pulled down, and with the other hand she pushed up on Tricia's elbow. The double grip gave her enough leverage to break Tricia's hold, and she slipped out from under the deadly headlock.

She floundered to the surface, lungs aching and bursting, and air had never before been so sweet and glorious. She sucked it in, feeling life return to oxygen-starved muscles. Her mind reeled under the dazzling light of sunshine and the heady feeling of freedom.

A boat was coming. But slowly, so slowly, almost as if it moved in slow motion.

My God . . . Tricia! Where was she? In her own desperate struggle for survival, Barrie's dazed mind had momentarily blotted out the other girl. Now she swam in a small circle, frantically searching for any sight of Tricia. There was noth-ing—nothing!

She dove under but in her exhausted condition she had to surface almost immediately. Her limbs felt leaden and she had to struggle to stay afloat. Water that had once felt so friendly and benevolent now seemed terrifyingly bottom-less, eager to drag her under. Her strength was fading as the boat pulled up beside her and strong arms hauled her aboard. Jordan's arms. She collapsed weakly against him. He helped her lie face down on the padded seat. His hand touched her back.

"She's conscious and breathing. I think she's okay." The voice seemed far away.

"Tricia!" Barrie gasped. "I couldn't find her . . ."

A splash as Jordan plunged off the boat. Barrie struggled to sit up, coughing and gagging from the water she had swallowed. Slowly her eyes focused on the figure operating the little outboard engine at the rear of the boat. Bill An-drews.

Barrie staggered to her feet. "I've got to help find Tricia!"

Bill grabbed and shoved her back to the seat. "No. Calm down. Jordan will find her."

Bill took off the shirt he was wearing over his swim trunks and slipped it around her shoulders. Until then she wasn't aware that the top of her bikini hung in tatters around her exposed breasts. Shivering, she clutched the shirt around her, needing its warmth as much as the covering for her exposure. The sun's brilliance seemed without heat.

Jordan surfaced, Tricia's head clutched under one arm. Bill maneuvered the boat alongside him. Together they got Tricia's limp body into the boat. Jordan climbed in after her. Bill headed the boat for shore, throttle wide open but progress still agonizingly slow.

Jordan's fingers gently searched the girl's throat for a pulse and then he immediately started mouth-to-mouth res-piration. *Oh Lord, don't let her die.* Helplessly Barrie re-peated the words over and over inside her head until they blended into one long word of prayer. Tricia was a strange, lifeless color, her sun-kissed hair unreal around her ashen face.

The engine coughed and sputtered. Jordan glanced up from his rhythmic efforts to revive Tricia. Bill fumbled with the controls, obviously uncertain what to do. Jordan would have to handle the engine. Barrie wobbled to her feet. She'd had training in mouth-to-mouth respiration, but had never worked on an actual drowning victim. But she had to do something! If only she could have held Tricia's head above water until the boat arrived. If only—

"I'll work on Tricia—"

"No, Sit down." Jordan's voice was curt. "Bill will do it. I'll see about the engine."

The men exchanged positions, clambering over Barrie as if she didn't exist. The engine died and Barrie felt a frustrated rage. Jordan fussed with something on the engine, all the while breathing curses, and finally the engine sputtered to life again. The small trolling engine, not meant for speed, seemed as helplessly impotent against the expanse of water as Barrie felt.

When the engine was running smoothly, Jordan finally glanced at Barrie. "Are you all right?"

"Yes. I swallowed some water but I'm all right. I—I tried to save her . . ." Her voice trailed off despairingly.

"It's too bad you didn't think about saving her a little earlier. Before she got so far from shore. What the hell did you think you were doing swimming out so far?"

"But I had no idea she was following me," Barrie protested. "She isn't an expert swimmer. It never occurred to me she'd try to—"

"No, you just wanted to make damn sure everyone noticed what a great swimmer *you* are! You always have to show her up, don't you? And you didn't give a damn if you risked her life doing it!"

Barrie stared at him in stunned horror. "Are you suggesting that I deliberately tried to harm her?"

"No. Of course not." His tone was contemptuous. He twisted something on the engine, desperately trying to get more speed out of it. "I'm just saying you were so wrapped up in proving your own superiority that you didn't give a damn about safety. Yours or Tricia's. You just didn't *care*."

"No . . ."

But even as she mouthed the word of protest against his brutal accusations, a flood of guilt swamped Barrie. She had gone after her swimsuit and returned with the deliberate thought in mind of outshining Tricia. She had deliberately shown off her diving skill, deliberately displayed a variety of swimming strokes that went far beyond Tricia's abilities. But she hadn't had any thoughts in mind of showing off or proving her superiority when she struck out for the center of the lake. She hadn't! She had only wanted to get away, to hide her tears.

But she should have noticed sooner that Tricia was following her. She should have used more care in trying to rescue her so the girl wouldn't have had the chance to drag them both under.

They were almost to the shore now. Everyone was crowding around on the dock or bank. Suddenly Tricia's limp body jerked and gagged in response to Bill's efforts at resuscitation. Her arms flopped and her eyes opened and rolled around vaguely. Bill helped her to a sitting position, and she leaned over the side and retched.

At the dock, someone gave Barrie a hand and helped her out of the boat. Jordan carried Tricia. Vanessa looked stunned, too shaken to do more than clutch the girl's still limp hand.

"She's coming around, but I think we'd better get her to a hospital." Jordan's voice was authoritative. People jumped to follow his barked commands to bring a blanket and his clothes, to clear out a space in the van.

Within moments, Tricia was stretched out in the van, Vanessa at the wheel. Barrie's last glimpse before the van door closed was of Jordan kneeling beside Tricia's blanketed form, his arms tenderly cradling her head.

Barrie felt lost, alienated from the people still milling around. They were all talking, asking each other how come no one noticed what was happening earlier. The women had been busy setting out food. The men had gone to carry another picnic table out from the garage.

"I thought they were just having a race," Bill Andrews's little boy piped up.

A race. Barrie felt ill. She dropped weakly to a chair. Bill Andrews came to check on her. She told him she was fine, though the words sounded foreign to her own ears, as if they were coming from someone else. She was still wearing his shirt. She looked around and finally found her jeans, but her blouse had disappeared in the confusion. Bill told her just to keep the shirt on and he'd get it some other time. She helped gather up the untouched food. In the late afternoon sunlight, the lake looked idyllically peaceful, but Barrie couldn't suppress a shudder as she looked at the glassy surface. She knew the terror that was just below that tranquil surface now.

Bill Andrews and his family gave her a ride in their station wagon to her cabin. They told her not to worry; they were sure Tricia was going to be fine. "She was conscious when Jordan and I put her in the van," Bill said reassuringly.

When they left, Barrie just stood there staring at the deceptively peaceful water. Never had she been truly afraid of the water, but she was now. She had only to look at it to feel it closing darkly around her, feel her helplessness against its relentless, suffocating power, know her own mortal vulnerability. And she could feel Tricia's terrified grip on her throat—

Her stomach churned in a sudden, sickening nausea, and she barely made it through the cabin to the bathroom in time. Her forehead was bathed in cold sweat when it was over. Her neck was painfully sore from Tricia's choking grip.

They should be at a hospital by now. Barrie kept seeing Jordan holding Tricia so tenderly in his arms, her head cradled against his chest. His ugly accusations rang in her ears over and over again until they blended into one long word like her silent prayer, but this was a word of brutal condemnation.

Didn't he know she had tried to save Tricia? Didn't he know that it was Tricia's frantic terror that had almost cost both their lives? No. And it didn't matter. All that mattered to him was that Tricia had almost drowned, and it was

Barrie's fault. Barrie's fault that the woman he loved had almost drowned.

Barrie stared unseeingly out the window as the truth dawned on her. That was what had happened. In those few minutes of terror, the truth had hit Jordan just as it now struck Barrie. He loved Tricia. The near tragedy had finally made him realize that. He loved her.

Barrie slumped into the blue chair. One part of her mind raged in angry protest. If she could only talk to him, tell him how much she loved him. . . . But another part of her mind echoed softly, regretfully, that it was too late. Perhaps it had always been too late for them. Perhaps it was better this way, at least for Jordan, for now he could love without suspicion or doubt, without ghosts or entanglements from the past. He and Tricia could go on to that shining golden future. Yes, it was for the best for him . . .

And yet Barrie wasn't quite saintly or noble enough to do more than recognize at the moment that the thought might be true. Perhaps someday she could resign herself to it, even accept it. But not yet, not yet. Barrie was fervently glad Tricia was alive and safe, and yet she had the dizzying feeling that it was *she* who was drowning now. Drowning in loss and despair, feeling life and hope drain out of her, as if she were sinking helplessly through translucent waters . . .

She raced outside, strangely gasping for breath. The sun was setting behind a bank of clouds, rimming them with a golden edge of light. The water looked dark and bottomless and evil.

No, no, it wasn't evil, Barrie tried to tell herself. It was just *water*—neutral, lifeless, with neither good nor bad intent. But she was afraid, afraid. . . . The water seemed to choke her even as she merely looked at it. She wanted to run, run so far she never had to see or fear it again.

Instead she forced herself to walk to the water's edge, to dip her hand into it and let the cold, clear liquid trail through her fingers. Suddenly she knew what she had to do, and if she didn't do it now she might never be able to swim again. She stripped off the jeans. She was still wearing the bikini bottoms underneath. She dropped the shirt, hesitating only momentarily when the torn bikini top fell with it. She had the strange feeling that if she didn't do this *now*, if she took even the moments necessary to go inside and change to a whole suit, she might never be able to force herself into the water again.

Even now she couldn't make herself dive. She slid off the rock into deep water. There was no shallow beach here. She felt pure terror as her feet dropped into nothingness. Her body felt rigid, leaden, as if nothing could hold it from sinking endlessly.

But she didn't sink. Automatically her muscles responded, moving in the familiar strokes and rhythms. Thankfully she paddled around, staying close to shore but slowly feeling her confidence returning. She also had to admit to herself that she hadn't always used the best judgment when swimming alone. It was foolish to swim so far out alone, as she often did, just because she felt safe and confident. Expert swimmers sometimes found themselves in trouble too. But the fear that had briefly paralyzed her was gone, and the water was a friend once more.

She was almost ready to get out of the water when a car pulled up in front of the cabin. Jordan! He was carrying something. Her blouse. He started toward the cabin, spotted her in the water, and changed directions.

"How is Tricia?" Barrie called.

"They're going to keep her overnight for observation, but the doctor didn't think there would be any complications." He stood on the rock, looking down at her in the water. "I brought your blouse over."

"Thank you. Just leave it there on the rock. Bill's shirt is there somewhere, if you'd like to return it to him."

She paddled slowly, waiting for him to grab the shirt and leave, but he just stood there watching her. With the sun gone, she was getting chilly, but she had no intention of getting out of the water in her topless condition with him watching. Her naked breasts suddenly seemed the coldest part of her. She carefully kept her body low in the water, conscious of the tautness of her nipples.

"Not everyone could enjoy a pleasant evening swim after what happened today. How nice that it doesn't bother you."

His voice was bitingly sarcastic. He obviously thought she was just enjoying herself in a carefree swim, unconcerned that Tricia had nearly drowned.

Well, what did it matter what he thought? Her explanation of how she'd had to force herself into the water would mean nothing to him. It suddenly occurred to her that this was just another weapon in the arsenal of reasons he was accumulating to justify dumping her. He had already blamed her for the near tragedy. Now he could hold a lack of concern against her too.

"I'd like to talk to you," he said. "Do you think you could spare a few minutes from your swim?"

Barrie ignored the still sarcastic tone. "There's nothing to talk about." She sidestroked out a few yards farther. "I believe you said everything in the boat this afternoon."

"Barrie, come into shore."

It was a command heavy with warning, but she ignored it. "No."

"Then it looks as if we'll have to talk in the water." He flung his shirt to the rock and unfastened his belt. Her eyes widened in alarm, but then she realized he was still wearing his swim trunks under the pants. He swam out to her in a brisk crawl stroke.

She eyed him warily, keeping herself afloat with a minimum of movement and effort. "I'm sorry about Tricia. But I was not out to prove my superiority or anything else when I swam out in the lake. It's just something I do when I'm—" she paused, lifting a hand out of the water to brush a dark strand of hair out of her eyes "—disturbed," she finished finally, for lack of a more evasive word.

"Disturbed?" His inflection made the word sound frivolous. "What was there to be disturbed about? You'd just impressed everyone with your fancy dives and proved your superiority over Tricia again. And don't tell me you didn't know *exactly* what you were doing then."

Guiltily, Barrie had to admit he was right about that much. "I'm sorry," she said unhappily. "It was a childish thing to do."

She was aware that the day's events and nerves and exhaustion were catching up with her. Reluctantly she swam to the rock and hooked an elbow over the edge for support.

"She tries to compete with you, you know." He gripped the rock only a few feet away from her. His face had a weary, almost gaunt look. "Don't you realize that?"

"Of course. I'm her idol," Barrie said sarcastically. "She wants to be just like me."

"Perhaps she does, though she'd never admit it even to herself." His voice was contemplative. "She's pretty and vivacious. But you're beautiful and sophisticated. She's bright—but you're talented. You have your stained-glass work and everyone is always complimenting you on it, and she is still floundering, wondering if she has any worthwhile talents or abilities."

"She made me look like a fool with that horse at the picnic!" Barrie flared angrily. "And she did it deliberately!"

"And she made herself look like a fool in that outrageous, sexy get-up at Vanessa's last night. You looked like a beautiful and supremely desirable lady, and she looked like a little—" He grimaced and left the word unspoken.

"You said yourself she looked very grown-up." Barrie had to grit her teeth to keep them from chattering in reaction to the chill seeping through her body.

"Barrie, she may *look* grown-up, but she's just an inexperienced kid off a ranch."

"And I'm a congressman's ex-wife. Fully experienced." Barrie's voice was bitter. "It's the first time you're ever suggested my background might be an asset rather than a liability." She moved her legs in the water, trying to stimulate circulation and warmth. Her arm was growing numb too, raised above her head so she could stay neck deep in the concealing water. Jordan was covered only to his chest. He looked as if he were prepared to stay in the water indefinitely. She suddenly felt infinitely weary. "Jordan, what does any of this matter? What happened today evidently made you fully recognize what your feelings really are."

He gave her a long, thoughtful look. "Yes, that's true. Perhaps I've been trying to avoid facing them."

"I'm sure it was obvious enough to everyone else last night how you felt about Tricia. You hovered over her like a jealous lover."

"I hovered over her, as you put it, because I felt she needed protection from that vulture Rayburn. Tricia was as far out of her depth at the party last night as she was in the water here today. Except that here the possible consequences were considerably more tragic."

"For which I am to blame, as you've made very clear." Barrie's voice was weary and bitter. "Does it make you feel better to heap blame on me? Does that somehow justify your loving her and not me? Jordan, you don't have to justify your feelings for Tricia. If you love her, you love her. Just leave me alone to—"

To suffer my broken heart in peace. But she didn't say the words aloud. Abruptly she shoved herself away from the rock and resolutely swam away from Jordan.

She didn't glance back and didn't realize he had followed her until a harsh hand clamped on her shoulder and roughly hauled her to a stop.

"Let me go!" She struggled under the unyielding grip.

"No. We're going to talk. You can swim back to shore under your own power or I'm going to drag you in."

She had a sudden mental image of his powerful arm dragging Tricia to the surface and knew his words were no idle threat. Reluctantly she turned and sidestroked back to the rock, but stubbornly she stayed beneath the water.

"Out," he said flatly. "We can't talk when we're both shivering."

"We were never that great at talking," she reminded him. Bluntly she added, "Our big attraction was always sex."

He reached for her, crushing her against his chest with a one-armed grip while his other arm holding the rock supported them in the water. She felt a small rumble of surprise deep in his throat as her naked breasts met his bare chest. His legs wrapped around her, holding her powerless as his mouth roughly found hers. His mouth felt cold at first, cold and foreign, but then a slow warmth began to flow between them. It came not solely from him, or from her, but from something generated between them, as if the contact created something that was more than the sum of the two separate parts.

Her ineffectual struggles dwindled. The warmth surrounding them melted through her resistance. The cold chill of the water receded into some far corner of her consciousness. She felt as if she were drifting in some tropical lagoon. Her passive acceptance of his kiss changed to a passionate return. Her arms lifted to encircle his neck, and her body melted against his.

When he finally lifted his head, his eyes caressed her face. She was unaware of her naked breasts floating gently in the water, the tips barely brushing his chest. His legs still held her in a sinewy prison.

"Is that what you meant?" His expressionless voice was at odds with the intimate touch of his body beneath the water.

Her eyes, dark as the water around them, looked into the blue-smoke depths of his. He spoke as if he were continuing a conversation she had started, but she couldn't remember what it was. His strong arm lifted her, and his head dipped to touch his mouth to the curving slope of her breast in a warm, damp caress.

"Don't—"

"Why?"

"Because you make me feel things I don't want to feel." She felt them now, an aching longing that brought a wildly reckless, all too familiar desire to seize the rapture of the moment and forget all else. He did that to her. In his arms, nothing else seemed to matter. And yet it did matter, she reminded herself fiercely. It did! She must not lose sight of that. "Jordan, I—I can't separate sex and love the way you do. It's tearing me apart when you do this to me." As if to prove her point, her body shifted of its own volition, meeting his in a new and even more urgent intimacy that turned her voice to a murmur of despair.

"You think that is what I do? Separate sex and love?"

"Isn't it?"

"Maybe it's what I tried to do."

On the surface their voices spoke this ordinary language of words, but beneath the surface of the water there was another language as his body sent age-old messages of desire and hers received and returned them. With a strength born of sudden panic, Barrie twisted away from him. She had to escape before it was too late, before the treacherous demands of her body overrode reason and logic. She scrambled out of the water and flung Bill's shirt around her naked shoulders. Without looking back, she fled into the house. Inside, she wrapped a robe around her shivering body. When he came into the shadowy room a few moments later he was also dressed. He was carrying her blouse and the ragged top of her bikini.

"Thank you," she said stiffly. "Now please go."

If he heard her, he ignored her request. "Barrie, I never told you much about my first marriage."

It seemed a strange subject for this particular time. "I don't think that matters now."

"Yes." There was a note of regret in his voice. "It does matter." Briefly, unemotionally, he told her basically the same facts Vanessa had revealed. The girl had married him on the rebound. She was still in love with the other guy, though she hadn't let Jordan in on that little secret until she decided to return to her first love, of course.

"It hurt, but—" He shrugged. "I got over it. And then you came along and I fell in love with you, and you did very much the same thing. There was your mother's interference, of course, but basically, Killian needed you and you went back to him."

Barrie couldn't deny that basic fact. But what none of his measured words expressed was the anguish she had felt, or that she had fallen in love with him too.

"By the time you came back here, I'd gotten over you." He hesitated, absentmindedly picked up a tool from her worktable, looked at it unseeingly, dropped it. "At least I thought I had. And I damn sure didn't want to be in love with you again. Or still. I figured I'd learned my lesson. *Twice*. And I didn't want to go through it again. I fought like hell against being in love with you."

And won, Barrie thought hopelessly. So now he was in love with a girl who had no past to haunt him. She tightened the belt of her robe around her waist. "Jordan, I—I'd really rather you didn't go into all the details of why you don't love me now."

"You think that is what I'm doing?" He'd been talking

to her from across the room, as if he wanted to keep a distance between them, but now he came to stand in front of Barrie. She folded her arms protectively in front of her. "Barrie, I wish you didn't have your past. I wish things had worked out right for us the first time. But even more I wish I didn't have *my* past, because I know it has made me suspicious at times when I had no right to be suspicious. But did you ever think that certain events in your past are reflected in how you think and feel now about me?"

Barrie looked at him wonderingly. Killian had lied to her and cheated on their marriage vows. Had she suspiciously looked for the same kind of behavior in Jordan?

"It would have been even more idyllic if we could have met and fallen in love a long time ago, before either of us had known pain and entanglements and unhappiness." He reached out and caught her elbows lightly in his cupped hands. "But life never makes things simple, and we can't live on wishes. We can't change the past, and we can't be rid of it. We can only accept life as it comes and go on from there."

Go where? Her eyes searched his wonderingly.

"Perhaps, for a while, I had one more wish," he admitted slowly. "I wished I could fall in love with Tricia. I wasn't blind enough not to see that she was—infatuated with me. I tried to love her but..." He shook his head as if it were a matter beyond his comprehension.

Barrie looked at him in confusion. "But you said that today made you realize how you felt about her."

"It did. And I was ashamed of myself." His hands tightened on her arms. "Maybe that is why I struck out at you the way I did. When I saw the two of you struggling in the water, I knew that she was pulling you under. And all I cared about at that moment was *you*. Only you. For a few moments perhaps I even hated her." He shook his head in remorse. "Afterwards I felt so selfish, so guilty for not caring more what happened to her. And so I lashed out at you, and accused you of not caring."

"You cared," Barrie said quietly. "You saved her life. I don't doubt you'd have sacrificed your life trying to save hers, if it came to that."

He nodded slowly. "No matter what I said in the boat, I know you came very close to making that sacrifice too. And somewhere in there it finally got through to me that the past doesn't matter. I love you, Barrie. Only our future together matters to me." His mouth dipped toward hers and then stopped, as if he suddenly doubted his right to her lips. Or suddenly remembered her bitter accusations. "All of you. Forever," he said softly. "I want to marry you . . . will you marry me?"

"I love you, Jordan," Barrie said simply. "I want to marry you—"

He smoothed the damp glossy hair away from her forehead. "I think I detect a *but* at the end of that sentence. Are you afraid I'll always be suspicious? That you'll always have to prove your love for me?"

"I love you," Barrie repeated. With nothing held back, she added, "I want to prove it to you. That's why I told Killian I wasn't interested in doing the restaurant murals for his friend. I didn't want the trip to come between us."

Jordan looked stricken. "No! You can't give up an opportunity like that."

"I already have." Her voice was serene.

He shook his head. "Why didn't you tell me? Why didn't you talk it over with me first?"

Her reply was simple and basic. "Because I didn't want to beg—or bargain—for your love."

His arms tightened around her until the grip was almost fierce. "I'm begging for your love," he said huskily. He shook his head again. "But I don't want your love for me to be a sacrifice. I love you too much for that."

Sacrifice? She saw the love and concern in his eyes and felt the fiercely protective circle of his arms. No, there was no sacrifice. "There will be other opportunities," she said softly. She smiled. "We'll blend our talents. You'll design houses, and I'll decorate them with stained glass."

"I have in mind that we might blend our talents in other ways too. Perhaps a bit more earthy ways." His voice was husky, but his sudden grin was deliciously, wonderfully wicked. His mouth touched hers with sweet fire. "We have a house over there just waiting for us to fill it with kids . . ."

Barrie reached up and locked her hands behind his neck. Until this moment she had not even known for certain he wanted a family. Her eyes searched his. What other wonderful delights were there to learn about him, this intimate stranger she loved?

She lifted her mouth to his, first step down that glorious lifetime road of living and loving, learning and exploring together.

WATCH FOR
6 NEW TITLES EVERY MONTH!

Second Chance at Love ™

_____ 06148-4 **THE STEELE HEART #52** Jocelyn Day

_____ 06422-X **UNTAMED DESIRE #53** Beth Brookes

_____ 06651-6 **VENUS RISING #54** Michelle Roland

_____ 06595-1 **SWEET VICTORY #55** Jena Hunt

_____ 06575-7 **TOO NEAR THE SUN #56** Aimée Duvall

_____ 05625-1 **MOURNING BRIDE #57** Lucia Curzon

All titles $1.75

WHAT READERS SAY ABOUT
SECOND CHANCE AT LOVE

"SECOND CHANCE AT LOVE is fantastic."
—*J. L., Greenville, South Carolina**

"SECOND CHANCE AT LOVE has all the romance of the big novels."
—*L. W., Oak Grove, Missouri**

"You deserve a standing ovation!"
—*S. C., Birch Run, Michigan**

"Thank you for putting out this type of story. Love and passion have no time limits. I look forward to more of these good books."
—*E. G., Huntsville, Alabama**

"Thank you for your excellent series of books. Our book stores receive their monthly selections between the second and third week of every month. Please believe me when I say they have a frantic female calling them every day until they get your books in."
—*C. Y., Sacramento, California**

"I have become addicted to the SECOND CHANCE AT LOVE books...You can be very proud of these books....I look forward to them each month."
—*D. A., Floral City, Florida**

"I have enjoyed every one of your SECOND CHANCE AT LOVE books. Reading them is like eating potato chips, once you start you just can't stop."
—*L. S., Kenosha, Wisconsin**

"I consider your SECOND CHANCE AT LOVE books the best on the market."
—*D. S., Redmond, Washington**

*Names and addresses available upon request